ONE-WEEK
ODYSSEY

ONE-WEEK ODYSSEY

A BLACKWATER LAKE COZY MYSTERY

CAROLYN BRODEUR

BELLE ISLE BOOKS
www.belleislebooks.com

ISBN (Paperback): 978-1-966369-31-8
ISBN (eBook): 978-1-966369-32-5
Library of Congress Control Number: 2025912678

Designed by Sami Langston
Project managed by Ashley Barnhill

Published by
Belle Isle Books (an imprint of Brandylane Publishers, Inc.)
5 S. 1st Street
Richmond, Virginia 23219

BELLE ISLE BOOKS
www.belleislebooks.com

belleislebooks.com | brandylanepublishers.com

CHAPTER ONE

"What can I brew for you today?" the barista asked.

"A medium cinnamon caramel latte, please," I replied, and wondered if I should make it a large instead.

"Great! We'll get started on that brew right away. What name can I use for the order?" the barista asked.

"Kat, with a K," I answered. She smiled and wrote the name on the cup.

"It'll be ready in a few. You can pick it up at the end of the bar," she said, and gestured toward the other end of the café.

I undoubtedly needed the caffeine tonight. I was going to a board meeting for the Southern Pines Homeowners Association. I was a portfolio manager for the Residential Service Agency, a company that manages multiple HOA organizations and condominium associations. This board meeting was for one of our largest clients, a community that served residents fifty-five years of age or older. The main topic on the agenda for this evening was the budget.

I thought back to earlier this afternoon; the board's treasurer and I had haggled on the phone up until the last minute. I had to rush out the door of my townhome for the meeting and barely had time to print the updated documents and get them to the board members. I felt my blood pressure rise as I scrambled to push the send button in my email.. It was then that I received a text message from that same treasurer telling me he would be late for the meeting because he needed to stop and put fuel in his car and air in his tires. I groaned inwardly.

At least the man is better at numbers than he is at remembering basic tasks, I thought.

Since the meeting couldn't take place without him, I knew that I would have at least an extra fifteen minutes to get things set up. I decided that I had enough time to stop for a coffee, it seemed a good idea at the time, but as my stress levels were still high, I was now second guessing myself.

Maybe I don't need the caffeine after all, I thought, too late.

Having placed my order and paid for my latte, I shuffled to the other end of the bar to wait. I stood there looking up at the café signage and wondering why the owners had named their shop "The Two Brewmsticks Cafe."

Their logo was charming. It featured a black cat sitting next to a steaming cup of coffee with a single witch's-style broomstick lying across the table—but it didn't match the café's name. In fact, the whole shop felt inconsistent with the modern urban neighborhood around it. It felt like it belonged to another time and place. It hadn't been in the shopping plaza very long, a few months maybe, and it seemed as if it had appeared by magic, out of nowhere. It was the only brick-front building on a street otherwise surrounded by glass and concrete.

Shrugging off these sentiments, I pulled out my phone. I noticed that I had another text message, this time from the board president giving me a heads up that one of our more difficult residents had announced on social media that they were coming to the meeting. I sent a thumbs-up to acknowledge the text and forwarded it to the security officer on duty for the evening. I sighed, closed my eyes, stepped aside, and leaned against the shop wall to wait for my coffee.

As I leaned back, my elbow bumped into a thumbtack on the bulletin board and knocked down a flyer. The bulletin board usually held posters about local events such as upcoming concerts in the park, dungeon and dragon nights, and church functions. The sign above the board indicated that it was strictly for community events, but I occasionally noticed a rogue business advertisement or job posting. This flyer was for the latter: an understated job notice designed in a large, blocky font. Normally I wouldn't have even glanced at it because it looked like someone had printed it at home, but the headline caught my eye.

Seeking Community Manager for Private Lake Community.
Excellent six-figure compensation and benefits.
Housing provided.
Email BlackwaterLakeHOA@mail.net with cover letter, resume, and portfolio of properties previously managed, including description of budgets, community size, and types of amenities.

That was it. It was brief and to the point. I thought about tacking it back on the bulletin board, but just as I was about to do so, the barista called my name. I absent-mindedly folded the paper and slipped it into my purse as I went to the counter to collect my latte. As I took that first sip and breathed in the spicy-sweet aroma, I immediately forgot about the flyer and my worries about tonight's board meeting.

I arrived at the meeting a little early, and the treasurer showed up only ten minutes late. We convened the meeting promptly upon his arrival. Surprisingly, the treasurer seemed well prepared. He was able to present the budget with little assistance from me. The troublesome member also made an appearance during the member-comment period of the agenda. Yet, contrary to the concerns raised by the social media rumor-mill, she only praised the board for planning to add six more accessible parking spaces near the pool.

Some of the Southern Pines Homeowners Association residents—"members," as the industry calls them—were cantankerous and difficult to work with. The luxury fifty-five-plus planned community had some retirees who seemed to have nothing better to do with their time than to meddle with the HOA and the management of their community. They "loved" their neighborhood the way a child loved their new, brand-name outfit on the first day of school, as a status symbol and a badge of honor. Thankfully the difficult members did not make up the majority, as most members truly loved the community and invested their time, talent, and treasure into keeping it running smoothly and looking beautiful.

Beauty was undoubtedly in the eyes of the beholder. Despite the inviting name of the community, there wasn't a single pine tree in the whole two-thousand-acre place; there were just uniformly shaped Bradford pear trees. They lined every street in a monotonous pattern, one in front of each one-story luxury home. Just like the tedious aesthetic of the community, this meeting was beginning to drone on. I found myself wishing for something interesting to happen. I even hoped that the troublesome member would cause a ruckus so there would be something to break up the staleness of the evening.

This was my sixth annual budget meeting since becoming the lead manager on the Southern Pines account, and each year had been mainly the same: crunch the numbers, haggle over the numbers, meet about the numbers, and get the board to vote on the numbers. Then another year would be spent trying to convince the board and the members that the numbers weren't arbitrary, and that they couldn't just blow the budget on new ideas and luxury conveniences.

The board soon closed out the agenda and wrapped up the meeting. I left the meeting tired and burnt out. I could barely keep my eyes open on my way home. I drove past the boring, invasive, lollipop-shaped Bradford pear trees and made my way out of the community. Somehow, I made it safely across the county to my townhouse.

Once home, I opened a bottle of wine and settled on the couch to listen to music before bed. My phone buzzed, and I jumped up to scramble through my purse, trying to find it before the call went to voicemail. Frustrated, I dumped out my whole purse and found my phone at the bottom. I was disappointed to find the caller ID indicated that it was nothing more than a robocall. I declined it and started to put everything back into my purse. That was when I noticed the job advertisement flyer. I picked it up and strode back to the couch, opening the browser on my phone, and entered a search for "Blackwater Lake HOA." There were several Associations with similar names, but none of them were in Virginia or anywhere near Centreville, where I lived. I had to believe that the ad was posted by someone local since it had been tacked to a bulletin board; if that was the case, why hadn't I heard of this HOA? The community management industry was not that big, and we often crossed paths with other managers at conferences or training events. I flipped the ad around in my fingers, idly fanning myself with it.

Oh, what the heck. Taking my glass of wine, I moved to my workstation and opened my laptop. I hastily whipped up a cover letter and emailed it, along with my resume and portfolio, to the address on the paper. I felt confident that nothing would come of the application, but I shrugged and finished my wine, then shut down the laptop and headed upstairs to bed.

The following day, tired from the late-night board meeting, I woke to my phone buzzing on my nightstand. I reached over, and noticed an unfamiliar phone number with a 540 area code and pressed the answer icon, mustering up my brightest, most awake voice and greeted the caller.

"This is Kat, how can I help you?"

"Hello, is this Katherine Normand?" A woman's voice asked.

"Yes, may I ask who's calling?" I said hesitantly. I was beginning to suspect this was a telemarketer.

"My name is Barbara. I'm the Human Resources and Administrative Manager for Blackwater Lake HOA. We received your resumé last night, and the board president would like to schedule a video interview with you. Would you have some availability this week?"

Stunned at the speed of the response to my application, it took me a moment to recover. But when I did, I readily agreed to the virtual interview. Then I went on to ask Barbara about Blackwater Lake.

"Where is it located?" I asked.

"Oh, in Virginia, down near Lynchburg."

"Wow! That's nearly three hours away; how did a flyer for the job opportunity end up on a bulletin board in Centreville?"

Barbara explained that the café in which I had found the notice was owned by a woman named Hetty Brown, who lived in Blackwater Lake. "Hetty owns another café in our town, the original Brewmstick Café. She had the foresight to post the job opportunity in their northern café despite the slim chance that anyone qualified would see it and be interested."

I was floored by the serendipity of it all. What were the odds of me finding such an ad in a café more than two hours away from where the job was located?

Barbara changed the subject to the interview, and we chatted about my availability and scheduling. She explained that if this interview went well, the next step would be to meet in person with the board president and some other board members and staff. She even offered to arrange for the in-person interview to be held at the Two Brewmsticks Café in Centreville since it was convenient for me, assuring me the other board members and staff would already be in Northern Virginia handling other business. I readily agreed and came away from the call with the impression that I was at least a shoo-in for a follow-up meeting.

Two days later, I was sitting in my home office wearing my second-best suit and slacks and waiting for the Zoom call to queue up. Once Barbara launched the call, she introduced board president, Clive Owens, who led the interview from that point forward while Barbara sat off to the side, quiet but fidgety. She seemed to be a bundle of energy, the opposite of Clive. Clive was genial enough; he seemed like a warm, friendly gentleman. He appeared to be in his sixties, African American, with a round countenance. He wore a V-neck sweater, collared shirt, and round gold wire-rim glasses that complimented his round features. He spoke softly, with a warm drawl that reminded me of my grandfather's Georgian Southern accent; it broke the ice for me almost immediately.

The interview progressed well. We discussed all the critical things that typically come up in a first-round interview: my experience, the list of communities that I have managed; and Clive in turn offered background information about the Blackwater Lake Association, such as the budget, community size, and amenities. The description that he gave made the subdivision and its surrounding town sound like a beautiful place to live, full of character and community. As with any interview for this level of position, Clive asked me some questions about how I would manage specific situations if I were to get the job. The first question, about how I would handle an inclement weather situation, wasn't unusual. However, the second question caught me off guard.

"What would you do if a large wild animal became a dangerous nuisance in the community?" His demeanor remained calm and gave no hint of insincerity. I started a bit and found myself answering a question with a question, which I try to avoid doing during interviews.

"Um . . . does that happen often? What kind of animal, a black bear?" I asked, trying to stall for time and get clarification.

"No, not a black bear," he said, evading the first part of the question. "It has happened once or twice in the past; an animal even broke into the clubhouse during a board meeting one time. So how would you handle it if it happened again?"

The question was odd; if it had happened once or twice before, some protocol must have been established for handling such a situation. Still, I didn't want to answer with yet another question.

"I would need to familiarize myself with the established response plan if there is one. I would probably contact the Virginia Department of Wildlife and Recreation—"

"Well, that would be a problem," Clive interrupted. "The DWR doesn't have any offices nearby, and they won't come out to our little town. They've pretty much told us not to bother calling."

I raised an eyebrow. The scenario was practically unheard of; if the state agency knew of a dangerous nuisance wild animal, they would certainly want to be notified and probably would get involved.

"Okay . . . then I guess I would send out a notice to residents, warning them to be wary of the animal. Perhaps we would cancel any outdoor activities and close the beaches and parks, depending on the nature of the animal. Ultimately, I think I would have to call in a trapper or a hunter to deal with it."

"Hmmm," he said, as if that was not the correct answer.

"As I said, it would be best to familiarize myself with the established protocol first," I hedged. Clive nodded in acknowledgment and glanced at Barbara.

Barbara then picked up the flow of the conversation and transitioned the interview to the next question.

"What would you say has been the most unusual experience you have ever had as a manager for HOAs?"

I had to think about that one for a minute. What did she mean by unusual? Did she mean strange or funny, or perhaps she meant some type of emergency? I decided to go with an amusing anecdote instead—assuming that the conversation about weather and animals had covered the handling of emergencies.

"Well . . . uh, the most recent unusual experience that has taken much of my time over the past few weeks involves birdbaths. A member of the community in question decided that all bird baths were toxic to birds and has advocated prohibiting them via the HOA's regulations. However, as one would expect, there are many bird lovers opposed to the idea. It's become quite controversial; social media pages were created, newsletters distributed, and debates held. I must say that it has become pretty heated for such an everyday topic." I cringed inwardly, hoping this story would suffice.

"Hmm . . ." she said, and the glint in her eye told me I had missed the mark. I fished around in my mind, trying to come up with the right story to share with them. Unbidden, a memory from my childhood came to mind; it's one that was often triggered by talk of unusual experiences.

"I do have another story; it's not one from managing homeowners' associations, but one from my childhood. I think you will find it interesting." Barbara glanced at Clive, and he gestured for me to continue.

"I grew up on a farm. It was small; we only had a produce stand, and some chickens and ducks for eggs. However, the land was once part of a much larger farm, built in the 1700s. I remember once, late at night, when there was a full moon, I woke up and looked out my window. Across the lawn was a grove of white pine trees that surrounded an old pile of rocks and dirt, which I had always assumed was debris from when my father built our house. Anyway, that night, I could have sworn that I saw a man in old-timey clothing and a wide-brimmed hat. I watched him remove rocks from the pile and line them up along the edge of the pond in front of our house. He appeared to be making a rock wall." I looked from Barbara to Clive, and I could tell, even via the video call, that they were engrossed in my story.

"I got out of bed and tiptoed to my parents' room across the hall. They were both sound asleep. I debated waking them to tell them what I had seen, but when I looked out their window, the man was gone. I decided that it must have been a dream, and if it wasn't, then nothing bad could come from someone randomly building a rock wall. Somehow, I managed to roll over and go back to sleep. In the morning, I checked the grove of trees near the pond. Sure enough, there was the beginning of a rock wall, a line of gray rocks that stretched for about six feet. I never did tell my father about it—I was sure that he would think I was crazy—and he never mentioned the rock wall, either." I concluded with another shrug.

"That was quite a story," Clive said—without judgement, as far as I could tell. From there, the interview veered back to more ordinary topics such as governance and community, my experience with communication methods, and other typical HOA management concerns. We concluded the interview on a positive note, and Barbara said that she would be in touch.

Three days later, I received another call from Barbara asking if we could schedule the in-person interview. I hesitated a moment before answering; that first interview had felt a little off kilter, and I wasn't actively looking for a new job. But general manager positions for large scale HOAs were rare opportunities in this field; career managers often found a good job and then stayed there until they retired., so I agreed to the second interview. Babs said it would take place at the Two Brewmsticks Café in Centreville also helped me feel a little more comfortable about the situation. While the café had only recently popped up in the shopping plaza near my subdivision, I felt very much at home there. I trusted it was a safe place to meet with a large group of strangers.

The café was charmingly rustic. The building felt like it would fit right in a more historic area, such as Old Towne Alexandria or Fredericksburg. Despite being new, the interior felt as if it was hundreds of years old; you could imagine historical figures such as George Washington or Thomas Jefferson meeting there for a cup of tea. Above the main floor was a mezzanine-level section that ran along the perimeter of the café, with enough charming little wooden tables and chairs to seat about twelve people. It was there that we met for the interview. Clive, Barbara, and the other three interviewers pushed a few tables together, and we gathered around with our coffees.

In addition to Clive and Barbara, I was introduced to Willow Hargrove, Director of Maintenance for Blackwater Lake HOA. Willow was graceful and tall; she was so tall that her head brushed against the low ceiling of the mezzanine. Her long black hair was neatly done up in braids. And her warm, golden-brown eyes seemed to have a fleck of green that caught the sun from the skylights above. She was one of the most confident people that I had ever met. When I ascended the stairs, she stood ramrod straight and offered her hand for me to shake, smiling so brightly that I was momentarily mesmerized by her brilliance. She seemed slightly ethereal, yet at the same time more present than anyone else in the room. A touch on the shoulder from Clive redirected my attention to the rest of the group.

Clive introduced me to the two other board members participating in the interview. They were both in their sixties and retired from working in the DC Metro Area. David Armstrong had been an engineer with the NASA Goddard Space Flight Center. Hillary Wen had worked as a staffer on the Hill for several different senators. They had both retired to Blackwater Lake within the past five years. As Clive introduced them, I made a mental note of their names and backstories. David was nice enough, if not very interesting, but Hilary gave me an odd vibe. She was strangely aloof one moment, then overly friendly the next, and her hot and cold attitude made me wonder if I had any chance of getting the job.

The questions were mostly mundane and followed the type of script one would expect for such a senior managerial position. It was only when Willow spoke up that the topic veered once again in an unusual direction.

"What experience do you have with rare and unusual flora and fauna? Our community is nestled deep in the forest, and we often encounter animals and plants that might not be found elsewhere."

I could tell that Willow thought that this question was rather proforma; she had asked it in such a nonchalant way. However, I couldn't help but think back to that first interview and the question about wild and dangerous animals.

"Well," I started, "my father was a certified wildlife rehabilitator. We often had rare and unusual animals on our farm that he would nurse back to health. Then he would work with the local conservationists to release them. My father was particularly adept at caring for bats, so we often had a wide variety of endangered or threatened bats in our care."

Willow beamed at this pronouncement.

"Oh . . . I love bats," she said. "They are so adorable. I regularly make sure that we have bat houses set up around the lake. They do such an excellent job of keeping the mosquitoes at bay. What about flora?"

"Like I said, I grew up on a farm. We grew produce and had a small farm stand. It was all pretty standard as produce goes. However, up on the hill on the west side of our property, under the grove of white pine trees, there was a small patch of lady's slipper orchids that I was very protective of. I'm unsure why; I was too young to realize they were a protected species, but I instinctively knew not to let my friends pick those flowers. I was passionate about guarding them too. Once, I pushed a friend down the hill because she'd insisted on picking one for her science fair plant journal."

Although it didn't seem possible, Willow smiled even more radiantly at hearing this story.

"You did the right thing!" she cried. "Lady's slipper orchids are very special; the Messengers need them to speed them along their journey."

"The Messengers?" I asked.

She blushed, apparently realizing that I didn't know what she meant.

"It's an old legend, about a race of Fae that use the magic of the lady's slipper orchids to complete their missions as messengers," said Clive, waving the conversation along without further explanation. I blinked and filed this information away in my mind for later.

Once again, the interview resumed the normal flow of conversation. We finished our coffees, shook hands, and parted ways. I felt light and giddy; I was excited about the community they had described and the scope of work that the job entailed. I knew that I was the right person for the job; but more than that, for some strange reason, I felt like I *needed* the job.

At home that afternoon, I immediately called my best friend, Penny, and told her about how the interview went and how I eager I was for the opportunity. To say that she was skeptical would have been an understatement.

"You can't be seriously considering this?"

"I am! When will I ever get another opportunity like this?"

"An opportunity to get stuck out in the boondocks of Virginia? Hopefully never!"

"The town of Blackwater Lake sounds lovely; it certainly does *not* sound like it's the boondocks! Plus, my gut tells me that this is something that I *have to do*," I argued, even though a part of me felt Penny might be right.

"Well, at least let me help you make a plan; that way, you have somewhere safe to return to if it doesn't work out."

"Sheesh, thanks for the vote of confidence," I snarked.

"It's not you that I don't have confidence in; it's this shifty redneck HOA that you seem intent on hitching your cart to."

"Rednecks? Really? You don't know anything about the people that live there. Anyway, like I said, I'm sure this is the right decision. It's like this job was created *just for me*. I just can't explain why." Deep down, I knew Penny was right to be worried, but I still felt that inexplicable urgency.

"That makes no sense. But I'm here for you and I will back whatever crazy decision you make," Penny said. I thanked her for her support and then headed to bed.

In the morning, I received a call from Barbara telling me they wanted to offer me the position. We briefly negotiated salary, but it was difficult to ask for better than what they were already offering. In addition to a six-figure salary, my benefits would include five weeks of paid time off and the use of a fully furnished lakefront house. I agreed, and by the time the phone call was over, I had an employment contract waiting for my signature in my email inbox. I signed the agreement, returned it, and gave my two months' notice to the Residential Service Agency.

CHAPTER TWO

Two months later, the gravity of the situation weighed on me more as I wended my way past the utopian, monochromatic houses of Southern Pines, with their pear trees and laurel hedgerows. This was my last board meeting as a portfolio manager. I would no longer have the backing of a large company to support me and to provide guidance and resources in managing my clients' accounts. I would be on my own. Not my own boss, by any means, but on my own to succeed or to fail as I saw fit. It was a nerve-wracking prospect.

I parked my car in the back lot behind the clubhouse and walked around to the main entrance. Being a fifty-five plus community, there were almost more accessible parking spaces than traditional spaces. It didn't matter to me; I always made a practice of putting members first, and I would have parked around the back regardless.

The building was your standard pseudo-colonial style with white siding, black roof, and black shutters. The style tried very hard to give the impression that the community was as old as some other historic buildings in Virginia, but the vinyl siding and shutters spoiled the illusion. Once inside, the building featured the standard hotel-style décor, with ubiquitous fleur-de-lis prints on the carpeting and over-stuffed furnishings. There was little charm or character about the place. The only unique item was the vintage pinball machine in the bar—an original 1960s Williams Apollo .

Community lore held that the developer of Southern Pines once owned several arcades up and down the East Coast, then shut them down and moved into the real estate business in the 1980s because Northern Virginia's population was growing so rapidly. He kept five pinball machines and installed one in each amenity at Southern Pines. The one in the pool and spa complex, an original Atarians model from 1976, had been his favorite, and rumor was that it may even be haunted.

As I walked past the pinball machine on my way to the main banquet hall, I ran my hand across its glass surface. I felt like doing so was a way to pay tribute to the original developer of this community, and that perhaps it would lend me a bit of good luck going forward.

In the meeting, I walked over to the dais at the front of the hall and took my seat at the end of the table. There was nothing for me to set up tonight. My replacement, Reginald Coldwater, had arrived a few minutes before me and had already set out the board agendas and attachments. He was young and had only been in the field for about five years, but he was more than capable of doing the job. He was just completing the setup of the PowerPoint and projector when I arrived.

For some reason, the board president, Rhonda St. James, had insisted on the pomp and circumstance of formally handing over the account from one manager to another. It was all rather silly; the Residential Service Agency hired the managers, and the contract was with the firm. Managers were interchangeable, more or less, and we often covered for each other when one was on vacation or un-available. We had regular team meetings and kept shared files for all required documents, notes, and community resources. The whole transition ceremony seemed superfluous to me, and the formality of the situation seemed to put undue pressure on Regi; I could see that he was sweating. The hall itself was cool; the air conditioning was in overdrive, yet I watched Regi wipe his brow on his sleeve. I felt a little bad for the guy.

Surprisingly, the entire board arrived on time, and we convened the meeting on schedule. We went through the regular process by rote and approved the agenda and the minutes. Then, before the member-comment part of the meeting, the board president present-ed me with a gift: my very own pear-shaped topiary bay laurel and a framed picture of the clubhouse surrounded by Bradford pear trees. It felt like a fitting end to such an anti-climactic job.

The board president next announced that Regi would be taking over as the portfolio manager. There was a lot of awkward hugging and handshaking, and then Regi and I traded places; he took my seat at the board table, and I took my leave of the meeting. I struggled back to my car, laden with the cumbersome potted laurel and large picture frame. By the time I got there, I was sweating just as much as Regi had been. *So much for an easy night,* I thought.

I shoved the plant and frame into the front seat. There really wasn't anywhere else to put them. My car was already packed for the move to Blackwater Lake. Most of my belongings had already been shipped to the lakefront home that the HOA would be providing. All that was left were the last-minute items such as clothing and toiletries. I had crammed them all in the trunk that morning, knowing I would have a limited time to do so tomorrow. Tonight was my last night in my townhome, and tomorrow morning, bright and early, I would be headed to Blackwater Lake.

As I pulled into my driveway, I glanced down at the plant, wondering if it would be okay in the car until the morning. It was late August, and although the night temperatures had started dropping, they were still in the mid-seventies.

"Sorry, Mr. Laurel, hopefully it's not too hot for you tonight. I promise that once we get to the lake house, I will find the perfect spot for you." I patted the top of the plant, grabbed my purse, and headed inside.

I tossed my purse on the dining room table. It wasn't a big house, just about twelve hundred square feet, but it was comfortable and was a place that I'd been happy to call home for the five years I'd owned it. I'd bought it as a short sale when I was about thirty-five years old and was so proud of myself for owning it. Northern Virginia has some of the most expensive real estate in the mid-Atlantic, so the fact that I, a single thirty-something, could own her own home there was impressive. Having lived in it for nearly five years, I had even built up quite a bit of equity.

I stood between the living and dining rooms at the bottom of the stairs and spun slowly around. The townhouse was still completely furnished. I had even upgraded my living room furniture, since my last set had been with me since college and had a lot of wear and tear. I would surely miss the place, but at least I didn't have to truly part with it. I had plans to rent it as a fully furnished home for traveling physicians.

I strode to the kitchen, pulled out a container of leftover chicken piccata, and heated it up in the microwave, sipping a glass of wine while dinner cooked. When it was ready, I sat at the kitchen table and scrolled through my phone absentmindedly while I ate. In my inbox, I came upon an email from Clive, the president of Blackwater Lake HOA. Upon seeing the email, my heart skipped a beat. Could something have gone wrong? I was sure I had squared everything away with Barbara; there really wasn't any reason for Clive to email me on the Friday night before I headed down to Blackwater Lake.

Pausing only briefly, I tapped the email and opened it, then let out a breath I hadn't realized I had been holding. Clive had just emailed me to remind me not to use the GPS on my cellphone because it probably wouldn't work that far out in the forest. The closer I got to the George Washington and Jefferson National Forests, the more likely I was to get lost. He'd attached a printable copy of a list of directions that I could use for navigation.

Sheesh, I thought, *I haven't used printed directions since MapQuest was a thing.* I sent the directions to my printer and heard it clunking into action. It was an old machine, and noisy, so I had no qualms about leaving it behind for future tenants to use.

I finished my glass of wine and dinner, hand-washed the dishes, dried them, and put them back in the cabinet. A cleaning crew would arrive in the morning before the new tenant moved in, but I didn't feel comfortable leaving the dishes and trash for them to handle. With that thought, I opened the cabinet under the sink and took the bag out of the trashcan. Tying the bag off, I walked out to the front of the house where my trash totes lived, screened from view by the front staircase, and tossed the bag in.

Outside, I once again paused to take in the familiar neighborhood. The crepe myrtles were in full bloom, as were the knockout roses planted along the walkway by the HOA. I looked around at my front walk and the plantings that were resplendent with pink and magenta flowers. It was just after eight p.m., and the sun had finally set. However, the clouds were still a vibrant pink, purple, and orange swash. I loved this small neighborhood. It was established enough to have mature trees blocking the view of the major roads nearby. I'd always felt as if I was in a suburban oasis rather than an urban townhome community. I took one last look around and trudged back inside. Had I made the right decision in accepting this new job?

Well, I thought, *you're here now, and there is no going back.*

I went upstairs to get ready for bed. I tossed my dirty clothes into the laundry basket and brushed my teeth. I checked everything in the bathroom and laid out my outfit for the next day: a pair of khaki cargo pants and a lilac polo shirt. Barbara hadn't specified that I needed to wear anything special; it was just my move-in day and not my first day of work, but I still wanted to look somewhat professional.

It was far too early to sleep, but I wasn't sure how to fill the time. Ultimately, I decided to play a game on my phone and listen to an audiobook. It was what I would typically consider a "lazy evening," but it was what I needed to settle my mind. I grabbed my earbuds from their charging box and swiped open my audiobook app. Popping the earbuds into my ears, I lay back on the pillow and tried not to think about the magnitude of the change I was about to undertake.

Despite the distraction of a book and a game, I was unsuccessful at curtailing my racing thoughts. The weight of the situation was finally starting to hit. A move to a new and unfamiliar area, deep in the woods and remote from everything I was familiar with. I wished that I'd had the opportunity to visit the community and see what it was like, but it had all happened so fast— ridiculously, improbably fast. I felt like there was something almost supernatural about the whole process, almost as if fate or a fairy godmother had intervened. There was no way that I could be this lucky.

What is wrong with me? I chided myself.

This was an incredible opportunity: a six-figure salary, a lakefront home, walking distance to my office, and what seemed to be a friendly and welcoming community, if the board members were a fair representation of the whole . . . yet the nagging concerns about the suddenness of it all kept my mind reeling.

I realized that my mind had drifted away from my audiobook, and I reversed it back to the beginning of the chapter. I would never get to sleep if I kept letting my mind venture down this path of doubt. I set the sleep timer on the audiobook, set an alarm for the morning, and played a game on my phone until I drifted off to sleep.

The following day, I woke early, showered, dressed, and began packing the last of my items. I was kneeling on the floor and peering under my bed when I heard the bedroom door open.

"What are you doing?" Penny asked as she entered. I bolted upright and cracked my head on the bedframe.

"Oww! I'm looking for my earbud. I fell asleep listening to my audiobook last night, and my left earbud has disappeared." I knelt on the floor and glared at her. "You could have given me a heads up that you were coming."

"I texted you a half hour ago," she replied.

I huffed in frustration, pulled myself up from the floor, and reached for my cellphone in the middle of the bare mattress. Sure enough, when I picked it up, it vibrated in my hand, indicating that I had a missed message.

"Sorry, I must have been in the shower then and didn't notice it when I got out. Help me move the bed so that I can find my earbud."

"Move that bed? It's solid reclaimed oak; it must weigh a ton. Just buy another pair of earbuds before you head out." She gestured at the bed frame.

"These earbuds cost a hundred dollars; I am not going to just buy a new pair."

"Fine, Plan B, then," she said as she reached down and lifted and tugged the memory gel mattress up and over the footboard. "There, go look now."

I leaned over and peered down between the mattress and the headboard. Sure enough, there it was on the bottom frame. I scooped it up and popped it back into its charging box.

"Are you all packed? Can I help you take anything out to your car?" Penny asked.

"I'm all set, thanks. All I have left is that laundry basket. I'll take that down and shove it in the back seat when I leave." She nodded in response. "You should see the gifts the HOA gave me at last night's board meeting; you'll never guess what they are," I added.

"Was it wine and a gift card? Or maybe flowers?"

"Well . . . flowers are a close guess, but close only counts in horseshoes and hand grenades," I quipped.

"I give up," she said, shrugging.

"They gave me an enormous potted laurel and a framed picture of the lane leading up to the clubhouse, complete with Bradford pear trees dressed in their springtime splendor of white."

"You're kidding!" She had heard me vent many times about the copy-and-paste community with its bland landscaping plan.

"Nope, not kidding, they're out in the car. I'd show them to you, but they're not that interesting."

"The cleaning crew will be here at nine a.m. to turn over the property," Penny said. "But it's not like you've really left them with anything to do. You didn't have to pre-clean the house, you know."

"I know, but I didn't want them to think I was a slob."

Penny sighed in frustration and shook her head.

"The tenant is scheduled to arrive tomorrow, and all the paperwork was settled yesterday via email. You have nothing to worry about; I will take good care of your home," Penny assured me.

"Thanks, this really was quite a miraculous arrangement that you set up," I said as I hefted my laundry basket into my arms.

"All in a day's work," she humbly boasted, and together we walked down the stairs and out to my car.

Penny and I had known each other since college, and I trusted her implicitly. She worked for Featherlight Realty, a firm that occasionally managed rental properties as well as home sales. She oversaw all the company's rental transactions, to include maintenance contracts and cleaning services. She would ensure that my townhome was well maintained, and I knew if there was any damage, she would work like a bulldog to get the tenant to pay for it. I wasn't too worried about damage, though. Penny had arranged a sweet deal for letting out my townhome, one that would ensure the tenants were reputable and responsible. She would also handle the HOA's tenant fee and registration requirements, as well as the county taxes.

As Penny and I walked out to my car, I briefly thought about how unbelievable this confluence of events seemed to be. It would have been difficult for me to choose to go off to somewhere so unfamiliar without knowing that I had a safe place to land if I decided that this new job wasn't for me. Knowing that my townhome would be there for me if I needed it felt reassuring. Even if it was occupied by a tenant, I could always stay with Penny until the lease was up and then move back in.

What were the odds of all this coming together so perfectly? I thought.

I shrugged off that surreal feeling and tried to ground myself. Surely, all of this was just a streak of good luck. Still, I had a niggling feeling that things were going to change soon, and not for the better. It was a feeling that I couldn't push aside, no matter how hard I tried.

Breaking this negative train of thought, I shoved the laundry basket into the back of my SUV and, after a few tries, managed to hip-check the door shut. I had packed the last of my belongings into the car; the movers had taken everything else earlier in the week. There hadn't been much for them to take since I was leaving the apartment furnished; just some personal pieces of furniture and other items that I hadn't wanted to leave behind. My car held all the other odds and ends.

"So, are you ready for this?" Penny asked, her blue eyes squinting in the sun. Her fair skin was already turning pink, and her coppery hair glinted in the bright morning light.

"As ready as I'll ever be."

"You know . . ." she hesitantly said, "I still haven't found any information about this community, not in the real estate listings, the tax rolls for the state, or any other credible source. I am really worried about you."

"Thanks, but I have a good feeling about this . . . sort of."

"What do you mean by 'sort of'?"

"Part of me has absolute confidence that I am making the right decision, and another part of me feels as if this is all some sort of leprechaun gold—here today, gone tomorrow."

"That's a good metaphor. Another one would be that you are getting sucked into some crazy cult. Don't drink any Kool-Aid if they offer it to you, okay? Promise me that you will call me once you get there and then every day for as long as it takes for me to feel that you're safe."

"I promise."

She leaned in and gave me a hug. "Take care of yourself, promise?"

"Promise," I said again.

I climbed into my car and headed towards Route 66 West, which eventually took me onto 81 South. I had a two-and-a-half-hour car ride ahead of me. Fortunately, it was a direct shot most of the way. Once I was on 81, I could just use my GPS until I reached Roanoke. Then it would be all back roads, and I would be stuck using paper directions and a hand-drawn map of the Blackwater Lake town proper. I felt like some sort of pioneer.

I connected my phone to the console and pressed play on my audiobook. At least I would be able to finish my book on the drive. Pulling onto the highway, I tried again to see if I could get my navigation to take me directly to my destination. I pressed the voice command button on the steering wheel and gave it the good old college try.

"Navigate to Blackwater Lake HOA."

"Navigating to Blackwater, Virginia. You will reach your destination in six hours and twenty-seven minutes," replied the cheery artificial voice.

"Cancel navigation!"

"Canceling navigation," the voice acknowledged.

I knew where the navigation had been about to take me, and it wasn't my destination. Every time I tried to search for "Blackwater Lake HOA," the only information that came up was for Blackwater, VA, an unincorporated town in the far southwest corner of the state, right on the Tennessee border. I knew from my interview with Clive that the little town was not the correct location. While

Blackwater, VA, seemed to have some interesting attractions nearby, including the Natural Tunnel State Park, Clive had quickly assured me that Blackwater Lake was "a much nicer place." I had detected some snobbery in his voice, and I wondered if there was some sort of rivalry between the two similarly named locations.

Penny was right; all my research and hers had yielded nothing. It was as if this place didn't exist. I couldn't fathom how a place could exist in this day and age and not be on the internet. How did the HOA market itself to potential homeowners? From what Clive said, the community wasn't developer-owned; in fact, it was nearly built out, but that meant that any home on the market most likely had to be sold through a realtor. Yet, Penny hadn't been able to find anything. Not a single listing on the market.

As I put the car in cruise control and continued the long drive, I felt that same knot of anxiety in my stomach. Was this all too good to be true? No one in the HOA industry had ever heard of such a well-paid position with so many benefits. There were questions about whether using a home that had been bequeathed to the HOA as part of the general manager's benefits package was even legal. Still, I ignored all the rational and sensible feedback that I had received from my colleagues and pressed on. I knew that I had to take this job, it was almost a compulsion. My friends and co-workers were well meaning, but in my heart, I knew that they were wrong. There was just something about this opportunity that made me want to take the risk; I shoved the doubt aside and engrossed myself in my audio book, the latest paranormal romance by Molly Harper.

It felt like no time had passed at all when my phone dinged, and I looked down at the navigation map on the screen. The map showed that I was just two miles from the back roads I would need to take to my destination. This was it. This was my last chance to turn around and go back home. Once I started navigating by paper, it would be considerably more challenging to retrace my steps and head back to Centreville.

As I approached the exit and slowed my car, a stag jumped out of the woods and onto the shoulder of the highway. I swerved briefly to avoid him, but he turned around and ran back into the trees. Once I returned my focus to the road and my destination, I realized I had automatically continued along the route and was now at the stop sign at the end of the exit ramp. I shook my head.

"Guess there's no turning back now," I said.

CHAPTER THREE

Thirty minutes into navigating by a paper list of directions, and I felt that all hope was lost. I was sure I had driven past the same hunting stand four times already. I pulled over onto the side of the road and grabbed my cellphone from the dashboard dock, trying fruitlessly to get a signal. I even held my cellphone up through the moonroof. Nothing, nada, nil. Not even a single bar.

I tossed my useless brick of a phone onto the passenger seat and reached for my bottle of water. I hesitated. Sure, I was thirsty, but I also knew that I would need a bathroom sooner or later. It was a gamble. Either I sat here slowly dehydrating, or I would have to run out into the woods and answer the call of nature. I had flashbacks to the days when I used to go backpacking with my father; men had it so easy. I banged my head on the driver seat headrest.

"Ghaaa!" I grumbled loudly, leaning back and closing my eyes. Just then, I heard some type of wild animal yowl in response. It sounded like a mountain lion, and it sounded close, reverberating through my open moonroof from just beyond the tree line.

I recalled the strange questions that Clive had asked about how I would handle an aggressive wild animal. I wondered if this was the same type of animal that Clive had referred to.

This is how I die, I thought. *Sitting in my car on the side of the road in rural Virginia with a nearly full bladder, an empty stomach, and early-onset dehydration.*

Out of habit, I reached for my phone hoping to get a signal to call someone or navigate by, and not surprisingly, there was still no signal. I chucked the phone back onto the seat.

I picked up the printed directions and the paper map I had ordered online before this trip and tried to trace my steps back to Interstate 81. There was something to be said about being Gen X; my childhood had given me the navigation skills needed to survive without GPS. I had spent many a road trip reading an atlas or maps I had picked up from AAA. I sat up straighter and scolded myself for being so ridiculous. *I can do this; I grew up with MapQuest!* My stomach growled and diminished the effect of my personal pep talk.

"That's it!" I cried and threw open the driver's side door.

I walked to the back of my car, opened the hatch, and placed one hand under the opening of the tailgate to prevent anything from falling out that might have shifted during my travels. The only things that started to tumble were the pile of bath towels. I caught them with one hand and restacked them with the other. Then I rummaged through my reusable grocery bags looking for a snack. I had brought a bunch of non-perishable pantry foods to restock my new home. Somewhere in one of these totes was a box of granola bars.

Why didn't I have the good sense to leave them up front? I thought. But it was nearly noon, and I was starving. I had swung by the Dunkin' on my way out of town and bought a coffee and a blueberry muffin, but that was hours ago. The sugar from the muffin had long since worn off, and the coffee was coming back to haunt me.

I finally found the granola bars. I shoved all my belongings haphazardly back into the cargo area. The messy situation irked me to no end. Usually, my skills at "travel Tetris" were a bragging point for me. I prided myself on the ability to neatly fit all my belongings into a tight space. But now, at this moment, stuck in the woods of Southwest Virginia, I couldn't have cared less. I wedged the last tote bag into the back and hit the button on my key fob to close the tailgate.

I trudged back to the driver's seat. I was tired, hot, hungry, thirsty, and *lost*. The granola bars would not stave off the hunger; the sugary, sweet, empty carbs would soon burn off, and I would be hungry again in no time. I would also continue to be thirsty, at least until I was inevitably forced to suck it up and use the latrine au-naturel. I nibbled slowly on the granola bar, hoping to make it last so that I could keep my mind off my bladder. While I snacked, I stared at the map and directions again, hoping they would magically make sense now. Instead, they began to swirl and waver in my vision. Before I knew it, I found myself nodding off and my head dropped to my chest. I jerked awake again, to what I thought was the sound of a wild animal. It was still midday, but I wouldn't feel safe falling asleep in the middle of nowhere if there might be large, predatory wild animals nearby.

Taking a gamble, I toggled my dashboard display over to the built-in compass. The directions read to head southwest on the unmarked highway for approximately fifteen miles. Presently, my car was pointed northeast.

How did I get so turned around?

Conducting a masterful three-point turn, I forced my car to do an about-face and headed southwest. It appeared that I had traveled about ten miles from the highway, give or take, which meant I was only about five miles away from the gravel backroad called "Blackwater Lake Boulevard." I set the trip odometer on my car and slowed to a crawl. I supposed that if I missed this turn, I would just follow my car's compass and head back east. I wouldn't stop until I hit a familiar highway, and then I could find my way back home.

Don't be absurd, I chided myself, *you've come this far; there's no going back.*

Sure enough, just as the trip odometer ticked up to 4.8 miles, I saw what appeared to be a wide gravel road. I knew it was what I was looking for because it was surprisingly well-maintained for being so remote. Someone had invested some time and resources into this road: it wasn't overgrown or filled with potholes, and a sizeable, corrugated metal culvert pipe ran under the gravel road parallel to the main highway. I felt lucky just to have found it. I doubted I would ever have seen the road if I hadn't been looking for it. Something about it made the eyes gloss over it, almost as if a shimmer of heat distortion disguised the entrance.

I turned my car onto the gravel boulevard and reset my trip odometer. I was now headed northwest. The directions said that I should continue on the gravel road for about eleven miles, and then I would arrive at the main street area of Blackwater Lake. I hoped this was the right road and that these directions were accurate. I didn't want to get more lost out here than I already was.

The going was slow. Although the road was well maintained and my SUV had all-wheel drive, my tires still slipped and spun from time to time on loose gravel. About fifteen minutes into the drive, I pulled over again. I couldn't wait any longer; nature was calling. I opened my driver's side door, hopped out of my car, and ran off into the woods. I found a wide, tall oak tree, ducked behind it, and did my business. I was just buttoning my cargo pants back up when I heard another vehicle coming down the gravel road from the opposite direction. It was a large silver pickup truck with a lightbar along the top. As it pulled closer, I saw it was marked "Blackwater Lake Police" along the side.

"Thank the gods!" I exclaimed, and walked back out of the woods toward my car.

The pickup truck slowed to a stop, and the man inside took a minute to chatter into his radio before he opened his door and climbed out. At first, the sun's angle made it difficult for me to see him, but when he came into view, my heart nearly stopped. He was incredibly handsome, and the way the sun lit his features made them glow.

He was just a little taller than I was and built lean and strong. His warm, chocolate-brown eyes reflected the sunlight and had little sparks of gold in them. And his eyelashes . . . oh my goodness, I never knew any man could have eyelashes like that. They were gorgeous; any woman would have paid good money to have those eyelashes. My eyes drifted lower on his face, and I realized that he had just the right amount of stubble on his chin, which seemed to be chiseled from stone. I blushed, embarrassed that I was so taken by his good looks.

Shaking myself out of my reverie, I scolded myself for being absurd; *Hunger must be playing games with my head.* I realized now that he looked tired and had dark circles under his eyes, and I worried about the officer. Had he worked a double shift or something?

"Ms. Normand?" he asked. I was startled to hear my name.

"Yes."

"I'm glad that I found you. Clive sent me out here to look for you when you hadn't arrived by noon." He offered his hand for me to shake. "Chief Baxter. Jay Baxter."

I wiped my hands on my pants and then extended my hand to accept his.

"Nice to meet you, Chief Baxter, and boy, are you a nice sight to see . . . ." I sputtered and turned red as I realized what I had said. "I mean—a sight for sore eyes. I was beginning to wonder if I would ever get to town."

"It's not much farther now, just about five minutes down the road," he said, taking no notice of my faux pas. "Why don't you just follow me the rest of the way."

"Thanks, I really appreciate it," I said. "It's so strange to be without cell service or GPS. I mean, I pride myself on being outdoorsy and all, and I did earn the orienteering badge as a Girl Scout, but still . . ." I trailed off, embarrassed at my own nonsense.

"Don't worry, there is cell service in town. Navigation is still a bit wonky, but you can make calls and access the internet from your phone. It's just out here in the trees that we have a dead zone." He gestured to the woods around us.

"Well, that's a relief. I was dreading the idea of reliving the late 1990s over again." He looked at me and squinted in confusion. "You know, with no cell service and only dial-up for internet?"

"Yeah, I guess it was rough back then," he stated flatly.

Sheesh, was no sense of humor a job requirement to be chief?

"Well, lead the way," I said, and got back into my car to wait while he turned his truck around, and we both took off down the boulevard.

CHAPTER FOUR

The boulevard, as it was called, finally converted from gravel into a nice, paved roadway. The street was lined with poplar trees, already turning a beautiful shade of gold even though it was mid-August. The tulip poplars dappled the road with shadow as the sun moved west in the sky. It was your quintessential American main street.

I found myself in awe as I drove. The beauty of the place and the old-fashioned feel made it akin to a historical landmark like Monticello or Mount Vernon. It could have been featured on that old TV show, "Main Streets and Back Roads," which had been one of my father's favorites. This was not a new city; it had roots, and it would be fun to get to know this place. I pulled my car into a parking space in front of the market, behind Jay.

"I figured you might want to order some groceries before you head up to the house," Jay said, approaching my driver's side window.

"What, like Instacart? You have that all the way out here?" I reached for my cellphone, intending to open the app.

"Not Instacart, no. A little more old-school. Just call Goldi's Market, and either Dale or Ginny will take your order. Their son, Ethan, will drive it up to your house for you."

A Mom-and-Pop market?

"Wow, that sounds so . . . um . . . charming," I said, fishing for the last word.

"Yeah, I'm sure it's not as high-tech or fast as Instacart, but it's much more personalized. Sometimes they even remember to bring you something you forgot to order. It's like they have a sixth sense or something. They really know every customer's needs."

"That's incredible," I replied both impressed and embarrassed by my assumptions.

"Well, sometimes, just occasionally, they may *forget* a part of your order too. Intentionally."

"Forget a part of your order? Why would they do that? I thought you said that they had excellent customer service?"

"Usually, it's something that they know you requested on impulse, something you didn't need, like a pint of ice cream or something."

"Well, that's no fun; I like my vices. I certainly don't need someone looking over my shoulder about such things."

"Mm hmm," Chief said noncommittally. "Anyway, just pop in there and place your order. Are you hungry? I can pick you up something to eat at Banjo's." He gestured up the street to an old-school Southern-style restaurant that looked like a cross between a diner and a soda counter. The brick building's aged glass front windows showed artful chalk drawings of people enjoying menu items. The sign above the red and white striped awning had a logo that read "Banjo's Diner" and featured a banjo, a cowboy hat, and a star over the J and the I where the dots should be.

"I'm famished," I finally answered. "Do they have a tuna melt?"

"Of course, the best tuna melts in town, served on rye bread. Do you want fries with that or greens?" he asked.

"I should probably go with the greens. I need something a little healthier; I just snacked on a granola bar on my way here."

I thanked him for helping me and offered to pay for lunch, but he waved me off and joked that I should consider it a welcome gift. I stepped into Goldi's Market and once again felt like I was stepping back in time—not quite to the 1700s, but perhaps to the 1960s or 70s. The cash register was old and ran manually, with not a single electronic component on it. There was no conveyor belt either, just a long countertop with a worn Formica surface. Instead of aisles of colorful, rainbow-like products, there were just some shelves and cooler spaces along the room's perimeter, with a few rows of barrels in the middle. I was suddenly grateful to be able to order groceries; it would take me a long time to figure out how to navigate this new place. I wouldn't even know how to begin shopping here. What brands should I buy? How would I even pay my bill? It didn't look like they had a credit card machine, and I certainly didn't carry cash with me anymore.

A curvy woman with wavy blond hair in a flannel gray plaid shirt and black denim pants approached me with a radiant smile.

"You must be the new general manager of the community," she said as she extended her hand for a handshake. "I'm Virginia Johnson; most people just call me Ginny." Her strong Southwest Virginian accent added to her charm.

I reached to shake her hand, but she pulled me forward for a quick embrace. She was warm and smelled like freshly baked bread. On impulse, I returned her embrace and then pulled away.

"Katherine Normand, but you can call me Kat." I returned her smile in equal measure.

"Well, Kat, step over here to my counter, and I will gladly place your grocery order. Here is a little checklist we use; just check off what you need, and we'll bring it to your new house."

I looked at the list; it reminded me of the generic notepads that my mother would buy at K-mart. The list featured product categories that you might buy at the grocery store but did not include any brand names.

"How do I let you know what brand I want?" I asked, confused by the simplicity of the list.

"Don't you worry about that. We know exactly what our customers need." I hesitated for a moment and then shrugged. It had been a lot of driving, and I was ready to settle into my new house. As it was, I still had some unpacking to do this afternoon.

"Okay," I said, "I assume you know the address of the location? Because, frankly, I haven't memorized it yet," I added, embarrassed.

"Yep, we've got you covered. Just check off what you need on that list, and I'll have Ethan bring it out to you before dinner tonight. Oh, and don't worry about the bill; we'll send you an invoice at the end of the month."

"Couldn't be easier, seems just like magic," I said, and picked up the pen.

"Something like that." Ginny smiled and winked at me.

I thanked her and ran through the list, checking whatever I needed. Bread, milk, cereal, eggs. I noticed several subcategories were missing. Usually, I would buy specific things, like English muffins, but the closest word on the list was "bread." I sighed, thinking that I might have to come back here and figure out how to shop at the store after all.

I finished the checklist at about the same time as the chief walked back in through the door with a paper bag of sandwiches in hand.

"Ready?" he asked, handing me the bag. "I can take you up to the house if you'd like. It's probably easier if you follow me."

"That would be great! Frankly, I'm just too tired to try navigating the rest of the way home."

"I'm sure you will find your way around here soon enough, but it's probably better if I escort you. Besides, I promised Clive that I would." He quirked a half smile, and for some strange reason, I felt my heart flutter along with the butterflies in my stomach.

What foolishness is this? We just met!

"Lead the way," I managed to say.

I tossed the sandwich bag onto the front passenger seat and waited for the chief to pull his truck onto the road, then I backed out and followed him. It wasn't a long drive.

The boulevard stretched for about a mile once we got past the downtown areas. There were rural properties along the way. A trailer here, a split ranch there, and even a log cabin or two. Farther back in the woods, barely visible through the foliage, I could see some hunting stands and some farmland. From my interview with Clive, I had the impression that Blackwater Lake was a reasonably well-to-do town. However, the more I learned about the place, the more I began to think that beauty and wealth were only surface deep. Perhaps the subdivision was as lovely as I was led to believe, but the surrounding community barely seemed to be able to support itself. If that was the case, then I was miffed by the fact that such an affluent community had isolated itself from its humbler neighbors.

What does everyone do for work around here?

Thank goodness I could keep my townhome available if I needed it. Even if I had to move in with Penny temporarily, that would be far better than finding myself homeless and without a job.

I gripped the steering wheel tightly and kept close to the chief's truck. I wasn't sure how safe I was in this town. I suddenly had the sensation of being watched. We pulled around the next bend, and I saw the gate to the community on the right side of the road. I breathed a sigh of relief and chided myself for building up such nonsense in my head.

The front entrance was gorgeous. A large fountain stood between the entry and exit lanes. Once we passed the fountain, we pulled forward to a guard house on the left or a member entrance with a barcode reader on the right. Chief approached the guard house and gestured to my car behind him. I pulled through with my window down, not sure what to expect.

"Welcome to the community, ma'am," the guard said, and waved me on through.

We drove through the gate and came to a four-way intersection. The main road curved off to the left or right, but a paved driveway continued straight ahead. The chief drove straight on, and I followed him up to a beautifully landscaped cul-de-sac. To the right of the cul-de-sac was the driveway for a parking lot, and to the left was a driveway that led off toward some houses. But the sight directly at the end of the cul-de-sac caused my breath to hitch.

It had to be the clubhouse. It was a gorgeous stone and log building with a central structure and a wing off to each side. A second-story wrap-around balcony bowed out in the front and was covered by the central roof peak. Behind the curved part of the deck were cathedral-high windows framed by glossy natural logs.

Each wing featured a pair of symmetrical gables on the second floor, and each wing angled slightly back toward the lake. I was so mesmerized by the view that I didn't realize the chief had continued along the driveway to the left of the cul-de-sac, and I nearly collided with a trellis leading to a garden and firepit. I jerked the steering wheel manically, pulled around the cul-de-sac, and headed down the driveway.

There were two or three houses off this little lane, and the first one on the right turned out to be mine. It was a classic, A-frame lake house with cedar plank siding. The front, or rather, the back of the house faced the driveway; it was clear that the house was designed with the waterfront in mind. It featured a small cedar porch with two Adirondack chairs on either side of the door, which was flanked with two windows and capped with a transom. The driveway was gravel, and there was just enough room for two cars to park in front of the split-rail fence that stretched from each corner of the house.

I climbed out of my car and reached for my phone and the sandwich bag. I stood there awkwardly with my hands full, gawking at the house. The chief stepped around his truck and stood beside me.

"This is where I'm going to be living?" I asked. It was within walking distance of the clubhouse, where I understood my office to be, and though the house was small, it was perfect. It was the very lake house that I had dreamed of owning.

"Yep, why don't I let you inside. We can return for your things, and I can help you unpack."

"Oh, surely you have better things to do than to help me unload all my junk," I exclaimed, blushing slightly at the messy state of my car.

"Nope. I'm technically off the clock as of two p.m., so I'm all yours," he said, without irony. I was pretty sure my cheeks were even redder than before. I took a deep breath and plastered on a smile, trying to be nonchalant but suspecting that I looked as maniacal as the DC comics character , Harley Quinn. All I needed were red and blue pigtails to complete the look.

"Thanks, that would be wonderful. But I should probably eat something first; I think I'm getting lightheaded," I bluffed, trying to draw attention away from my erratic behavior.

"Of course." He pulled a pair of keys out of his pocket; they were on a leather loop keychain with the words "Majik Majestic" embossed into the leather. I wanted to ask what that meant, but I was too eager to see the inside of this beautiful place I would call home for the foreseeable future.

We walked in through the front door, and Chief Baxter handed me the keys.

"This is your set for the house."

I took the keys from him and nodded my thanks. As we entered the hallway, I noticed a door to a small bedroom on the left. The bedroom had a single twin bed, its head angled toward the window, with drawer storage underneath to economize the space. On the other side of the room was a small writing desk. The ceiling sloped upward, and several model airplanes were suspended near the top. I could faintly see that a mural had once been painted on the wall; it had been in a vintage style and featured images from the age of flight, along with clouds and birds carrying banners. Someone had halfheartedly painted a layer of white over it.

"This room is adorable. Why would anyone try to cover up that mural? I can only imagine how much work went into creating it!" I exclaimed.

"I'm not sure," said the chief. "The mural was from the original owners, who bequeathed the property to the HOA. I think this room belonged to their son."

We stepped back out. Across the hall was a small bathroom with a glass shower stall, and the next door down from that was the small laundry room. Emerging from the hallway, we entered a beautiful open floor plan. The kitchen was to the right, with a large skylight and two counter-height stools pushed under a generous butcher's block island in the middle. The countertops were likewise made with thick butcher's block, and the cabinets were done entirely in shades of white. At the end of the island was a small four-seater table, and to its left was the sliding glass door that led to the deck.

Opposite the kitchen was a seating area with a softly upholstered sofa and two basket chairs set up against the stairway railing. The sofa faced a television mounted on the wall across from the kitchen. A cast iron pellet stove sat at the end of the room, near the dining table and sliding glass door.

I stood in the middle of the room and spun around, walking slowly toward the counter to put my phone and sandwich down. I imagined my sandwich was cold by now, but I still stalled. I couldn't get over the massive windows that looked directly at the lake. The rear deck was huge and tastefully furnished with dark brown and tan wicker furniture. A brown deck box to one side doubled as a bar-height table. On the other side was a grill and a stainless-steel prep counter, beneath which I saw a small refrigerator and beverage cooler.

"You should really eat; there'll be plenty of time to explore the house." The chief opened a few cabinets and pulled out one white ceramic plate and a small salad bowl. He unwrapped the sandwich and took the greens out of their container, generously pouring the dressing on.

"Here," he said, "you look like you are about to faint."

I sat at the counter across from where he stood. He leaned back against the counter near the soapstone sink. *A soapstone sink! I've always wanted one of those,* I thought, and took a bite of my surprisingly still-warm tuna melt.

The sandwich had been wrapped in foil-lined paper, which kept it nice and toasty. It was delicious. I moaned indecently and threw my hand up to my mouth in embarrassment. However, the chief didn't seem to notice. He had taken his phone out of his pocket and was busy scrolling through it.

"Oh! You have service," I nearly shrieked in delight. I picked my phone up off the counter to look at the screen. I had full bars. I couldn't recall if I had noticed that in town or if it had just kicked in once we got into the community. Still, I was grateful to know I would have full connectivity here.

I noted that it was nearly two thirty p.m. How the heck had time flown by? I certainly hadn't been lost for that long. I had two missed calls from Penny and about a half dozen text messages from her. The last text message threatened that if she didn't hear from me soon, she would call the governor and ask him to rally the National Guard for a search party. I typed out a quick message to her.

"Arrived safe, my new house is gorgeous . . . and so is the chief of police." I knew my phone would be ringing momentarily, but I put it on silent and stuck it in my pocket.

Shoving one last bite of my sandwich into my mouth, I mumbled through my mouthful, "I've got to see the rest of this house." I wiped my mouth with the paper towel the chief had handed me when he set out the plate. "Have you ever been here before?"

"Not since the original owners were here. The last manager was a local, so he didn't need this house. It has been pretty much mothballed for about five years since the original owners passed away."

"Why did the last manager leave?" I asked.

"Well, he didn't. He's been missing for about four months now, presumed dead."

Halfway off the counter stool, I staggered in surprise at this statement.

"What?! What happened?" I asked.

"We're not sure. We've been investigating since the night he disappeared, but we haven't found any new leads yet. It was on May first, the night after the Annual Meeting of the Membership. He had given his usual speech; the same one he had given every year for the past decade. Then he got in his car, presumably to drive to his home on the other side of the lake, and was never heard from again."

"Oh, my gourd!" I exclaimed.

"What?"

"Sorry, force of habit; it's an expression I picked up from my grandmother. But seriously, you have no leads, not one?"

"We found his car, but that was it. It was abandoned at South Beach, left running with its door wide open. There had been a rainstorm that evening, so there were no discernible footprints in the sand. It was a dead end." He shrugged.

"Someone should have told me this story before I moved out here," I nearly shouted.

"Well, don't worry about it, we've got it covered. We will discover what happened to him; we believe it was an isolated incident; you have nothing to worry about."

"I certainly hope you have it *covered*, that's a rather disturbing story."

"We do, I promise. Let's check out the rest of this house," he casually said, changing the subject.

We walked up the switchback staircase to the second floor. The loft area was above the first floor's bedroom/hallway/ bathroom area and had a railing that overlooked the open living room below. Two more basket chairs looked out into the space below from the small lounge area. We walked toward the back of the house and through a small hallway into the master suite. On the right was a full bathroom with a clawfoot tub, stand-up shower, and an exquisite vanity. On the left was a walk-in closet. There were skylights in every room, even the closet. In the master bedroom was a beautiful, Amish-style pencil-post bed with its headboard against the bathroom wall. On the opposite side of the room stood a chest of drawers and a chaise longue.

Finally, at the very end of the room was what I had taken to be a window from the ground level, but was in fact a pair of bi-fold glass doors that opened to a screen on the other side. The doors and skylights gave the room the impression of being almost entirely open to the forest and sky beyond it. Even the view of the driveway didn't detract from the impression of being up in the trees.

"Wow," the chief said, "this is a really nice place. It looks like you'll be very comfortable here."

"Comfortable! I might never leave, not even to go to work," I blurted out.

"I'm pretty sure that would void your employment contract, but I could be wrong since I don't know the particulars."

"Nope, it would totally void my employment contract, but who could blame me? This place is heaven." I looked around the room and into the closet and noticed that all of my belongings had been unpacked and put away neatly. Whoever the association had hired to handle the move was truly professional; not a single item seemed out of place. Upon inspection, I saw that everything was exactly where I would have put it if I had unpacked it myself. On top of that, they had made the bed up with my own sheet set.

"Who did they get to move my stuff here, elves?" I asked rhetorically, not really expecting an answer.

"Maybe," the chief said, sounding fully serious. "Let's go get the last of your stuff so you can settle in."

As we walked down the hallway, the doorbell rang. Just outside the door was a young man, about seventeen years old, with his arms full of paper bags.

"Hey, Ethan," the chief greeted the boy.

"Got the groceries for the new manager," he muttered.

"Just put the bags on the counter in the kitchen; I can put them away when I come back inside," I directed.

The kid somehow managed to shrug while holding two over-loaded paper bags, then wedged his way in between the chief and me. I noticed that the trunk of his ancient Buick sedan was open, and two more bags were in the car.

"Should we help him?" I asked the chief.

"Nah, the kid's got it. Let's get you moved in."

We hustled out to my SUV, and I gingerly opened the hatchback. However, all the care in the world wouldn't have prevented the avalanche that ensued. Towels, a duffle bag, and a pile of pillows spilled out onto the gravel.

"Oops." I blushed again, but the chief seemed to take no notice and just began picking up the items off the ground.

"Where do you want me to put this stuff?" he asked.

"Upstairs on the bed; I'll put it away tonight."

He heaved his armload of my things and returned to the house, passing Ethan on the way. I began picking up my share of towels and blankets and watched as the kid grabbed the last two bags of groceries and went inside. I followed him into the house and dumped everything onto the couch.

"Thanks, Ethan," I said. "I'm sorry, but I don't have any cash to tip you with. Can your mom add it to my tab? Is twenty percent okay?"

"No tips," he grunted, and then walked out the door. Did he mean that he was upset because I couldn't give him a tip, or that they don't *bill* people for tips, or that he *couldn't accept* tips? I shook my head; I would figure it out the next time I placed a grocery order and make it up to him.

The chief and I had my car unpacked in a jiffy, and I shook his hand and thanked him for the personal welcome to the town. He took off without a glance back at me.

That evening, I lay sprawled out on the four-poster bed and stared at the night sky through the skylights. I had called Penny and was currently holding my phone at arm's length so that the shrieking voice coming through the speakers wouldn't deafen me.

"The least you could have done was CALL ME! You promised you would," Penny shouted.

"I know, I know, but it was all just a blur." I had the glass doors wide open. It was still summer, and the temperature outside was nearly eighty degrees, but the mornings were starting to feel cooler, and I knew that sleeping with the doors wide open would be perfectly comfortable.

"And then you have the nerve to drop me a text that says the chief of police is gorgeous—and then you don't answer your phone!"

Penny would never let this one go, but I knew what I had been getting myself into when I sent the text.

Once I had taken the time to unpack, put my belongings away, and shower, I'd crashed on my bed and finally called her. I told her all about the news of the disappearing manager. As expected, she had freaked out, insisting I pack my belongings and move back to Centreville immediately. I managed to talk her down, but then she berated me again for not calling her when I first arrived.

"So, what do you think happened to the previous manager?" she asked when she had finally stopped shouting.

"I have no idea. Honestly, it bothers me that no one told me about this."

"Of course it does, you nincompoop! It should bother you. See, I told you that this whole thing felt wrong from the beginning. Now you have a missing manager on your hands," she groused.

"It's not on *my* hands," I replied. "The chief is investigating; I'm sure he will find out what happened to Mr. Odeon. I can't imagine this man's disappearance has anything to do with me," I said, trying to convince myself as much as Penny.

"That's stupid," she said bluntly. "There's a good chance that it has everything to do with you; perhaps someone wants your job, or there is some corruption in the HOA. You could be thrust into the middle of something dangerous without knowing what is happening."

"I'm sure it's not that bad," I said, shrugging. In the background, I heard a buzz from the other end of the phone call.

"Hey, I've got to go," she said. "My laundry. Promise me that you will call me tomorrow. Promise!"

"Okay, I promise," I said, raising my hand in a vow even though she couldn't see it.

"Before noon, or I send out the National Guard."

"Before noon," I promised.

CHAPTER FIVE

On Sunday, I lay in bed listening to a pair of cardinals chirping in the crepe myrtle just below my window. They seemed alarmed and were chittering away something fierce.

I pulled myself out of bed, walked over to the screen, and looked down to see a chocolate brown dog with long, floppy ears and a glossy head of curly fur. Even from this angle, I could tell that it was likely some kind of spaniel. I threw on my sneakers and ran down the stairs and out the back door. As I stepped outside, I saw the spaniel playfully barking and trying to get at the cardinals in the tree. He didn't seem to want to catch them; he just seemed to like the sport of barking at them, but the cardinals clearly weren't having anything to do with this game.

I leaned down, grabbed the dog by the collar, and pulled it up onto the porch.

"Hey pup, cut that out. Let's get you some water," I said, struggling to redirect the dog's focus. He grudgingly acquiesced and turned his head to the hose and spigot that I had turned on. He thirstily lapped up the cool water from the hose, splashing almost as much as he drank.

I scratched him behind his ears and then reached down to see if I could find a tag on the collar. Sure enough, there was a bright red one with the name "Jet" engraved on it.

"Hmm. Jet," I said, and his ears perked up.

"Well, Jet, I don't see a phone number on your tag; you may as well come inside until I figure out what to do with you. I can't have you harassing the cardinals."

He happily followed me inside, his head held high and his tail wagging.

Now that I looked closely at him, I concluded he was a traditional, tri-color springer spaniel. His muzzle had a white line that began on his forehead and spread into a white delta around his nose and mouth. The white fur on his chest, legs, and belly was flecked with chocolate and black. He looked up at me adoringly as we stood in the middle of the hallway.

"What do I do with you?" I asked.

His ears perked up again, but of course he didn't offer any suggestions.

"C'mon, I haven't had breakfast yet. Are you hungry?"

He yipped in response.

We bustled into the great room, and he ran over to the couch and hopped up onto it, making himself right at home. I shook my head. Had there been anything about pets in the lease agreement for the house? Ultimately, it didn't matter; as soon as I found the owner of this pup, I'd get him back in their care.

"Cheese omelet?" I asked him, and his tail thumped against the couch in delight.

I took the eggs out of the refrigerator and hunted through the kitchen to find what I needed. I hadn't thought to ask for pantry staples such as olive oil or salt, but just as Chief Baxter had said, the grocers seemed to have guessed everything I'd forgotten. Surprisingly, they hadn't forsaken the two quarts of ice cream that I had remembered, nor had they forgotten the wine. I'd been secretly afraid they would be some sort of "food police" and wouldn't bring them. But no, they had brought mint chocolate chip, black raspberry ice cream, and four bottles of a local red blend wine. I was amazed at the quality of everything.

I warmed up the oil in the pan and then added the scrambled eggs. When the eggs began to firm up, I sprinkled some Colby Jack cheese into the middle and then folded it over. I cooked it just a bit longer to let the cheese melt, then smoothly scooped the omelet out of the pan and onto a plate, before cutting it in half and putting the second half onto another plate. As I placed the plate on the floor next to the counter, Jet hopped off the couch, sniffing the air in anticipation. Surprisingly, he ate the omelet daintily, nibbling it a bit at a time instead of scarfing it down all at once. I was impressed. I sat at the counter and ate my own breakfast with slightly less care. I was starving.

I glanced at my phone and noted the time: just a quarter past nine. Even though Penny had said to call her before noon, I knew she wouldn't be up until at least ten a.m. on a Sunday, and even then, she wouldn't answer the phone until after she had her first coffee. The best thing I could do in the meantime was make some coffee for myself and prepare for the day. I would have to find out who Jet's owner was, but I would rather be showered and dressed first since that might involve seeing actual people.

I looked around the kitchen for the coffee maker and realized there wasn't one on the counter, just a tea kettle on the stove. I began to open one cabinet after another in a frantic search to find the source of my caffeine fix. There had to be a coffee maker somewhere; knowing just how amazing the market was, I was confident they wouldn't have sent a bag of coffee if there wasn't one in this house. Finally, I opened the end cabinet on the island; inside, I found a French Press, a burr grinder, and an airtight canister for storing grounds. I took out the French Press, filled the tea kettle, and grabbed the bag of coffee. Sure enough, it was whole-bean, not ground. The process was slower than my Keurig, but I grudgingly admitted to myself that I could probably get used to it.

I found a ceramic travel tumbler with a lid. Once the coffee was ready, I poured it into the cup, noting that this roast had a sweet aroma already. Sweet enough, in fact, that I tasted the coffee black, which I usually would not do, and decided only to add a little bit of milk and no sweetener. Looking at the bag of coffee beans again, I saw that the brand was called "Blackwater Coffee," and the roast was called Hive Vibe ("a light roast of Guatemalan beans with a natural flavor of honey!"). I had a feeling it was custom roasted right here in town by the proprietors of the Brewmstick Café. I sipped my coffee and took a deep, relaxing breath, inhaling the vibrant, sweet fragrance. I felt a pair of eyes on me and looked down to see that Jet was transfixed with my every action.

"Well, boy, better get this day started so we can find out who you belong to."

I climbed the stairs to my bedroom and pulled out an outfit for the day. Jet had followed me, but as I started to undress for the shower, he turned out of the room and went back downstairs. I shrugged; he couldn't get into much trouble down there. I hopped into the shower, quickly washed my hair and body, popped back out again, and dressed in a denim skirt and a flowy but comfortable short-sleeved shirt. I didn't bother to blow dry my hair; I never did if I could help it. Instead, I just pulled it back into a ponytail while it was still wet. It would have a dent if I decided to take it down once it was dry, but I didn't care.

Back downstairs, I found Jet sitting patiently on the sofa again; his front paws were crossed, and he looked like he didn't have a care in the world. I wondered if I should try to call the police department to see if they had an animal control officer, or if there was a better number to call. I knew from all my research about this place that I wouldn't be able to find any information online. Before he'd left the night before, the chief had pointed out a custom magnet on the fridge with a list of the town's emergency numbers. Since 911 only sometimes worked out here, he'd explained, the HOA had distributed the magnets as an educational marketing piece a few years back. I looked at the list now, and I saw fire and rescue, police, the local doctor's office, and the numbers for the utilities.

I was just about to call the police department when I heard my doorbell ring. I scooped my cellphone and coffee tumbler off the counter and walked down the hallway to see who was there. Jet barked just once as I headed toward the door, but a glance out the door window showed that it was only Barbara. She had her hands full with a basket of goodies and had somehow managed to free up a finger to press the doorbell.

"Barbara!" I exclaimed as I whipped the door open. "Let me help you with that."

"Call me Babs, and thanks," she said. "It's a Blackwater Lake HOA tradition that we welcome newcomers with a basket full of local sweets, eats, and drinks."

I hefted the basket out of her arms and carried it down the hallway, plunking it on the counter. Babs followed behind me and then froze as she caught sight of Jet.

"Jet!" she scolded. "What on earth are you doing here!"

"Oh good, you recognize him. Do you know who his owner is? I found him by my back door this morning barking away at the cardinals in the crepe myrtle."

"I recognize the scamp," Babs said vaguely. "I'll see to it that he gets home."

"Thanks," I said, gratefully.

Babs walked over and tousled Jet's fluffy brown ears.

"So, are you excited to start work tomorrow?" she asked.

"I guess so, but excited might not be the right word. Nervous would be more accurate."

"You'll do just fine. Clive wouldn't have hired you if you couldn't handle the job. He's a good judge of character." She went over to the basket and pulled out a chocolate hazelnut truffle. She unwrapped the gold foil and popped it into her mouth. "Besides, you've got me to help get you started; what else do you need!" She smiled and pointed a thumb at her chest, then asked, "How'd you like the house? Have you seen the lake yet?"

"The house is amazing; everything I could ever have hoped for. As for the lake, I saw it from the deck and the upstairs windows, but I haven't really gone down to look at it."

"Well, there's no time like the present. Let's go check it out together." As she walked to the sliding glass doors, Jet seemed to know what was happening, and he jumped off the sofa and ran right after us.

"I guess he wants to come, too." I smiled down at him.

"Of course he does; he's always up to something in the lake," she grumbled.

We stepped onto the deck and followed the switchback path to the water. There was a small deck with two more Adirondack chairs and a dock that went out about ten feet into the water. A kayak was on a rack off the side of the deck, and some life vests sat on hooks nearby. Jet bounded onto the dock, skipping and leaping most of the way. He was so energetic that I felt sure he would either fall or jump off the dock, but since he was a local dog, he probably knew what he was doing. Babs and I sat in the Adirondack chairs, and I sipped my coffee, suddenly feeling like a bad host.

"I'm sorry, I should have offered you some coffee. I can go make you some if you would like."

"Nah, I'm good; that chocolate was enough to rev me up for the day. Any more, and I'll be pinging off the walls." She waved away my offer.

We sat for a few minutes in surprising silence, because I wasn't sure Babs had a "quiet mode." The only other time I had seen her this quiet was when she'd let Clive do most of the talking during my first interview. Every other time we'd spoken, I barely got a word in edgewise. I looked out over the lake. It was large enough that I couldn't see the farthest edge from where we sat. Beyond the forested banks rose tall blue mountains, rounded by age and covered in trees. Some of the trees were already starting to turn, showing hints of red, gold, and yellow, just tiny specs of color in the distance now, but a sign that summer was ending. The place was quiet, with no whining power boats or jet skis, airplanes flying over, radios, or music blasting from people enjoying their day. It was a little eerie. I decided that now was as good a time as any to get something out in the air.

"Babs, can you tell me about the previous manager? The chief says that he's missing and presumed dead. I can't believe that nobody told me about this!" I tried to keep my frustration out of my voice.

"Well, gosh darn it. I can't believe he's already told you about that. That man has terrible timing. I guess the cat's out of the bag now; I may as well explain. On second thought, I may have that cup of coffee after all."

"Oh, no you don't. You're stalling; get on with it. You should have told me about this from the get-go, or at least once you offered me the job so I could make an informed decision."

"Fine. . . ."

And in a stream of conversation that was more like one long run-on sentence, she told me the whole story. Apparently, the previous general manager, Arthur Odeon, had been the community manager for about ten years. Babs gave me the impression that he was neither liked nor disliked, simply a figurehead for management, and that the various board presidents ran the show. I groaned silently at that information, not liking the implication; either this board was hoping that I would be another such figurehead, or more likely, Babs was the glue holding everything together. Either way, it meant that I would have to navigate some stormy waters when it came to relationships with my colleagues.

Babs said that Mr. Odeon had been acting progressively stranger over the six months before his disappearance. He would come in late, leave early, claim to go to one amenity or another to check on something and then never show up there. On more than one occasion, he had been spotted on his boat in the middle of the workday, not doing anything remotely related to management but seeming to drive aimlessly toward the middle of the lake. He was spacy, often daydreaming or humming a tune to himself. She said it was always the same tune, but it wasn't one that anyone recognized. His behavior was so alarming that Clive had taken him aside and told him to get his act together.

"Was Mr. Odeon married? Did he have any kids or family? Did anyone think to talk to them about his behavior?" I asked.

"He was divorced; his wife moved out about a year ago. They never had any kids, so he was pretty much on his own at that time."

"What happened next? How did he disappear?"

"That's the thing, no one really knows. I was working on getting everything together for the annual meeting. The room was set up, the A/V system was in place, and his speech was prepared. Well, it was almost the same speech he gave every year, so by "prepared" I mean I had a copy printed out for him to review, just in case. He seemed to be a little more focused in the days leading up to the meeting, but I was too busy with the preparations to really give his behavior another thought."

I nodded encouragingly, and she continued.

"The meeting went off without a hitch. He gave his speech, the new board members were elected, and Clive gave awards. Then everyone went to a banquet to eat, drink, and be merry. Odeon left the festivities early, claiming he had a headache and just wanted to go home to bed. As far as I know, he got in his car, left, and that was it. Willow, our Maintenance Director, found his car the next morning when she was doing her rounds. She said it was just sitting on the beach, door wide open, soaking wet from the rain, still running, and nearly out of gas. She hollered for him and then tried to call him on his cellphone; she found it ringing in his passenger side footwell. Then she called the police." Babs finally paused for a breath.

"That's it?" I asked.

"Well, no, of course not. The chief and his guys went over the scene looking for evidence, and then we formed a search party to look through the woods in the area closest to the beach. It had rained that night, so any footprints had been washed away, but they found his watch on the beach near the water's edge. It was a smartwatch, you know, the kind that can track your steps and show you your text messages. But that was all they found. There is no other evidence anywhere. The police are pretty certain that he swam out into the lake. Suicide." She casually dropped this last sentence into the conversation.

"But why do they think it was suicide? Was there a note or anything to suggest it? Did they search the lake for him?" I asked.

"No note, but the chief and Detective Daniels think his erratic behavior suggested it was likely. Also, he hadn't ordered groceries in over two weeks. His refrigerator was almost empty, and he had barely anything in his pantry. And yes, they searched the lake, sent divers out and everything."

"That's so weird. I don't know the guy, but it feels like it's way too soon to say that this was a suicide. There's got to be more to this story. What triggered his odd behavior? Was it the divorce?"

Babs scoffed at this idea.

"The divorce, goodness no! Arty was thrilled about the divorce; he and his ex-wife had had a tumultuous relationship from the get-go, and according to him she was a bit of a leech. She spent all of their money on her ridiculous pet birds—thousands of dollars every year."

"Did something else happen? People don't just change their behavior for no reason at all."

"To be honest, once his wife left, he pretty much kept to himself. He had nothing left to complain about, so he didn't share much about his personal life. Who knows, perhaps he had a new girlfriend, and she dumped him." Babs shrugged as if this was all no big deal.

At that moment, Jet ran back along the dock; he was chasing a dragonfly and nearly leaped into my lap to pursue it. I put my hands up to block him from doing so.

"Jet! Be more careful," Babs cried. "We'd better get you home." She stood up and began walking back up to the house. Both Jet and I were caught off guard by her abruptness and froze in place.

Barbs spun around on the heels of her white slip-on sneakers and stood there looking stern, hands on her hips.

"Well, c'mon."

Jet took one wistful look at me but then ran up the hill to Babs. I quickly got up and followed her, grabbing my now empty coffee mug. We marched back up to the house, and when we got inside, Babs turned around and looked at me, finger pointed to the ceiling as if she had just had an epiphany.

"Almost forgot," she said. "Just walk to the clubhouse at nine a.m. tomorrow. The office is through the first doorway on the left and down the stairs. Sadly, we're in the basement; we've gotta keep all the nice areas for the residents. Ta-ta!" She waved at me and headed out the door with Jet hot on her heels.

After she left, I called Penny to catch her up on all the new details about the missing G.M.

"So, what are you going to do about it? The chief and detective clearly don't know what they are doing. It's obvious that there's foul play. Doesn't the chief report to you? You should make him open the case back up," she rambled.

"Again, I'm not going to do anything about it. It's not my job. And no, the chief does not report to me. I know it sounds strange, but there is actually a mayor in this small town. The chief answers to him."

"Why would they need a mayor when you oversee 90 percent of the town?" she asked, perplexed.

"I don't oversee the town, just the HOA, the amenities. The mayor manages the roads, fire department, schools, and utilities. You know that."

"I guess, but I just figured since it was such a small town and the HOA was so big, perhaps the structure was a little different."

"Thank goodness it's not. It may be a small town, but almost five thousand people live here. I couldn't imagine being responsible for all those services in addition to the HOA; it's enough to manage six beaches, a clubhouse, a community garden, four parks, two pools, pickleball/tennis courts, and a golf course. Seriously, Penny, I'm not sure if I'm cut out for this. I'm beginning to have my doubts about tomorrow."

"Well, don't worry, that's just first-day jitters; you'll do fine." And with that, we easily drifted into the type of conversation that old friends have, not really anything you would write home about, but familiar and comforting. I left the phone conversation feeling calmer and began to flit around the house, tidying up last-minute things, doing some quick laundry so I would have an outfit to wear, and just generally relaxing in my new home.

CHAPTER SIX

The next morning, I was up earlier than I needed to be. I could have rolled out of bed at eight a.m. and still had enough time to get ready for work, but I had tossed and turned all night and found myself wide awake at five a.m. I took a long shower and tried to settle my nerves.

I spent considerably more time getting ready than I usually would. When I had asked Babs what the dress code in the office was, she had given me the non-descript answer of, "Business, but with a relaxed, lakeside style," whatever that meant. So, I opted for a light blue linen blouse, tan wide-leg trousers, and a cute pair of soft gray flats. I went for a minimalist look with simple jewelry, an understated gold necklace with a single pearl, and a matching cuff bracelet, and pulled my hair back in a partial updo. I'm normally a no-frills kind of girl, but I wanted to make a good impression on my first day.

I kept my breakfast simple: eggs with cheese and toast. I had considered forgoing my coffee because I was worried about it causing jitters, but I knew that since I didn't sleep well, I would need a boost. When all was said and done and I was ready for work, I looked up at the clock, and it was only about seven-thirty. I still had over an hour to go until I had to leave for work. I decided to head out anyway. Surely someone would be at the clubhouse, since the restaurant opened for breakfast at eight. I figured I might as well introduce myself to some of my new staff.

Babs had said there was a trail through the woods that led directly to the clubhouse. I walked out the front door with my phone in my hand and my purse slung over my shoulder, and found the trail about fifteen feet away. It was well maintained, with crushed gravel and wide gradual steps bordered by pressure-treated wood. I was glad I had worn ballet flats instead of sandals. I probably would have ended up plucking gravel out from between my toes once I got to the clubhouse, and that was not a look I wanted to present on my first day.

As expected, the walk took just about five minutes, before I knew it, I was standing before that remarkable clubhouse building. I briefly admired the architecture; the wooden log structure almost glowed in the morning light, its rustic character offset by the careful detailing the architect had put into the balcony, windows, and design. I must have lost track of time, standing there absorbed with thoughts about how excited I was to work in such a beautiful place, because someone stepped up behind me and tapped me on the shoulder.

"Hey there, Kat, welcome."

I spun around, and there was Willow, my new maintenance director, smiling her thousand-watt smile. She looked ready for the day, dressed in a black polo shirt, light gray cargo pants, and a pair of steel-toed boots.

"Willow, what a wonderful surprise. It's so nice that you are the first person I see today," I said sincerely.

"Are you lost?" she asked. "Can I help you find your way down to the office?"

"That would be great."

"Of course! I was headed there anyway; I need to pick up a package that was delivered yesterday afternoon. C'mon, I'll show you the way." She strode with confidence and pride into the building. It was all I could do to keep up with her long gait.

Inside, the clubhouse was just as impressive as the exterior suggested—walls of windows framed with honey-colored wood; slate, tile, and hardwood floors that gave the place a feeling of durability and beauty; cathedral ceilings with a modern lighting scheme that blended with the traditional country lodge style. There was a hand-carved granite fireplace, and the furnishings were rustic but somehow modern. In one section, nearest the fireplace, were two sofas and two armchairs with ottomans, all upholstered with what looked like butter-soft brown leather. The banisters were made with laser-cut iron panels that featured a woodland scene, and the handrails showcased more of that smooth honey-colored wood.

"This is remarkable. You have done such a wonderful job maintaining this place! Is it hard to keep it so clean and in good repair?" I asked Willow.

"Not really; I have a good crew. Everyone brings certain skills to the table, and ultimately, we get the work done in no time."

I stood looking around in awe for a few more moments; then, without another word, Willow led the way to a wide, carpeted side staircase and down to the lower level. Babs had called this area "the basement," but that description couldn't have been further from the truth. Entering the office through a set of beautiful French doors, I found the area just as stunning as the main common areas upstairs, with plush wall-to-wall carpet everywhere you looked. Either Babs was jaded, or she really didn't know what she was looking at; there wasn't a cement floor or cinder block in sight.

To my surprise, Babs was already sitting at her desk in the main office, reading a book. I smiled brightly and stepped forward to greet her, then froze when I saw what she was reading. *The Art of Managing Up: The Definitive Guide for Managing Difficult Employers.* I tilted my head in confusion, much like I'd seen Jet do yesterday.

Finally, Babs looked up at me and smiled politely. She wore a flannel shirt with sleeves rolled up to the elbow and a tank top underneath. Her short-cropped hair was still primarily gray, but today it had a streak of purplish-blue. My confusion must have been evident on my face, because Babs stood up and came around from behind her desk. That's when I saw the rest of her outfit. She was wearing what could only be described as a denim skort, although it was more shorts than a skirt, and on her feet was a pair of Birkenstocks.

"Good morning, you're here early!"

"Yeah, I wanted to get a jump on my day and get to know my new staff," I said. "Willow ran into me out front and was kind enough to show me the way down here."

"Good morning, Babs," Willow said in her melodic voice from behind me.

"Morning, Will," Babs said in a monotone.

"Oh, do you prefer to be called Will?" I asked politely.

"No," Willow said flatly and glared at Babs.

"It's just a little joke between us."

"It's your joke, and you've never let me in on why you find it so funny," Willow said brusquely. "Anyway, Kat, so glad you are here. I've got to get back to work. Babs, have you seen my package?"

"It's in the copy room," Babs said, pointing to a closet behind her desk.

Willow disappeared around the desk and returned with a long, slender box that looked like it could hold something about the size of a baseball bat.

"What's in the package?" I asked.

"Oh, just some pest control stuff." She shrugged and headed back upstairs.

I felt the need to chide Babs about what appeared to be her incessant teasing of Willow, but I refrained. Prudence was the better course of action; I needed to observe their interactions more to see if this was a regular thing. Although Willow was annoyed, she didn't seem mad, and Babs seemed unperturbed by Willow's attitude.

"Oooh, I'm so excited. I can't wait to show you your office," Babs said, nearly bouncing on her heels. She was several inches shorter than me and had a round physique, though she was not overweight. Once again, I was caught off guard by her attire.

"Babs . . ." I said tentatively, "what exactly did you mean when you said that the office dress code was 'Business, but with a relaxed lakeside style'? Do you always dress so casually?"

"What! Oh no, of course not. No, no, no. I'm just headed out to lead a kayak lesson later this afternoon. I told the waterfront manager, Donny, I would take out one of the groups." She waved off my concern and then walked to the back corner office.

Not knowing what to say, I followed her. The door to the office was made of frosted glass that had been carefully etched with some kind of ancient boat surrounded by dolphins. Above the boat, etched in careful detail, was a flock of birds. The whole image was surrounded by an intricate pattern of grape vines. Distracted by the door, I realized that Babs had been talking to me, and I brought my attention back into focus.

". . . no one really knows why Arty had this design etched into his door, but he spent a pretty penny of his own money on it." She opened the door with some fanfare and stepped back to let me in.

My eyes grew wide as I took in the sight before me; I was so astonished that I nearly tripped over my feet walking into the room.

"What do you think?" Babs asked.

"This place is incredible!" I exclaimed. But "incredible" didn't even come close to describing it. The office was a long rectangle with two walls of windows. A large conference table made of a shiny wood that might have been reclaimed ship decking took up the better part of the room; on the short wall nearest the end of the table was mounted a good-sized smart board. At the other end of the room sat a sizeable desk made of the same age-polished wood as the table. In front of the desk were two visitor chairs upholstered with more of that butter-soft chocolate brown leather. The chairs were trimmed in a small diameter braided rope that appeared to be from an old sailing craft, weathered but still in good condition. The windows on the long side of the room looked directly out at the lake. I could see a beach, a dock, and some picnic areas. It was a beautiful view, and clearly, the office was in a premium location within the building.

The long, wall-side of the room featured a triptych of large canvas panel paintings, depicting an ancient Greek maritime legend. The artwork was extraordinary and appeared to represent *The Odyssey*. The first panel featured a ship full of men at the oars struggling to control the craft as a cyclops hurled rocks around them. The second and largest panel was reminiscent of a work by John William Waterhouse: it showed Odysseus lashed to the mast as sirens, in their bird-women form, attempted to lure him to his demise. The final panel showed the ship teetering on the brink of a whirlpool, overshadowed by a terrifying six-headed serpent. I shook off a chill that the artwork had inspired and moved to take in more of the room.

I walked over to the window and stood in awe of the beautiful view of the lake with the hills in the background. A colorful Sunfish was sailing out on the lake and an older gentleman was fishing off the wooden bulkhead to the left of the beach. The scene was so tranquil. I truly hoped that I would never take it for granted. I reluctantly turned away from the window and looked back at Babs, speechless; Babs seemed to have a perpetual knack for understating things. Even as I thought this, she again felt the need to apologize for something that wasn't a problem.

"Unfortunately, the clubhouse restaurant's deck is above your head, so sometimes you hear people walking or dancing up there; and if you work late, you will probably hear music," she said, as if this detracted from the ambiance.

"I don't mind that; I'm good at tuning out the noise. My college dorm was near a train station, and there was also a bar right by it. It's been a while, but I can channel the skills needed to turn all those distractions into white noise."

"Well, if you don't like the décor, we can probably change it. I would have to check with Willow to see if she has any wiggle room in her budget for redecorating. Frankly, Arty was the one who chose this motif, and he only had it installed about six months ago. I never really understood it. Sure, it was water-related, but ancient Greek ocean themes don't really jibe with lakeside views."

"No. It's fine, really. I don't mind at all, and I would hate to make such purchases so soon in my management of this community. This is fine. Perfect, even!" I protested.

"Okay, just let Willow and me know if you change your mind. We can help you get what you need. Unfortunately, being so remote, we can't just order from the big online stores; we will need to custom order anything you want."

"Really?" I asked incredulously.

"Yep, I know that you had difficulty finding this place with a map; imagine what Amazon or UPS goes through . . . to be blunt, they don't even bother. We have a drop shipment location for the town in Covington, and the local post office sends their trucks there to pick up everything . . . and I mean everything. Anything from furniture to clothing—most people avoid ordering online if they can help it."

"That sounds like a logistical nightmare; who assembles the furniture or installs appliances if the big box stores can't deliver here?"

"Oh, Ethan from Goldi's might do it sometimes; other times, it's Brian from the hardware store or some other guys in town looking to pick up a few hours. We have to be pretty self-sustaining around here, so people get work where they can."

"I was wondering about that; what people do for work around here, that is. Anyway, thank you for showing me my office. Can you show me where to find the files, budget documents, rules, regulations, and such so I can get up to speed with everything? Oh, and how do I get logged into my computer?" My thoughts began to race again as my mind ran through all the logistics that I needed to take care of just to get settled in, never mind what I would need to take care of once I had my bearings.

"Don't worry about the computer or the files; you can handle those things tomorrow. I have an appointment with Ned from IT for you first thing tomorrow morning. Clive is coming here at ten to give you a tour of the community and introduce you to as many staff as possible."

"Remind me again how many employees we have?" I asked. She had told me during the interview process, but with all the stress of the transition, the numbers had slipped my mind.

"We're the largest employer in the area, if you don't count the military compound just to the north of us. We have thirty full-time employees, sixty regular part-time, and in the summer, we add another twenty-five seasonal positions."

"That's impressive; how will I keep track of everyone?" I said, more to myself than to Babs.

"You'll be fine; we try to keep our contingent of employees around a hundred and fifty people or fewer. You know, Dunbar's number, we find it's the most effective way to ensure good communication."

"Uhm . . . Dunbar's number? I've never heard of that."

"Yeah, it's the idea that humans only have the capacity to maintain stable relationships with about a hundred and fifty people. I read about it in a management book once and talked Arty into implementing it here. Seems to work," she said, and shrugged.

Now that she described it to me, I realized that I had heard of Dunbar's number before, but the article that I had read said that the number also includes personal relationships, such as family or close friends, not just co-workers. By her logic, our number of employees should be much smaller, but I wasn't about to disabuse her of the idea; 150 people was as good a number as any to cap our employee count.

"Interesting," I replied, "well, I'll have to come up with a memory technique of some sort; I am not very good at placing names with faces."

"I'm sure you'll come up with something. Let's head upstairs to the restaurant and grab a coffee; I told Clive we would meet him in the lounge by the fireplace."

We bustled back out through the office and upstairs, doubling back across the building to the southwest corner again.

The restaurant was called The Roanoke, and its logo featured the restaurant's name carved into a tree. The interior looked newly furnished, as though they'd recently redecorated. All the furniture was well coordinated to give the intentional impression that someone had raided their grandfather's attic. It was not unattractive but rather homey and comfortable: an assortment of earth-toned leather chairs lined the bar and clustered around high-top tables, both round and square. There was one long rectangular table intended to host larger parties. The furniture styles were modern but paid tribute to old colonial pub styles and took inspiration from some of the historical houses in Virginia.

Babs led me to the breakfast service, noting that it was just a coffee bar on weekdays. There was a cabinet with some baked goods; a cooler with yogurt, milk, orange juice; and a basket of fruit. Payment worked on the honor system: all you had to do was walk up to the kiosk, key in your pin number, and select what you wanted from the digital menu. The items would be billed to your account and directly debited at the end of the month. I was impressed; it was a modern convenience for such a rural location, but the cost savings on staff were apparent. The kitchen staff and managers were already at work prepping lunch, and until then, all they had to do was check that the station was full, clean, and in good condition from time to time.

We grabbed our coffees, and Babs keyed in her pin number. When I offered to pay her back for the coffee, she waved me off and said it was no big deal.

"When was this space renovated?" I asked.

"Last year. C'mon, I'll show you around here while we wait for Clive," Babs said. She showed me the clubhouse's two lounge areas first: one featured a bar, sofas, and a fireplace, and the other had billiards, foosball, and shuttlecock tables. The main floor also housed The Shopette and the banquet hall/event space. She introduced me to the young shopette manager, Alice French, and then we went down the other set of stairs to the right of the front entrance.

These stairs led to a larger part of the "basement" than what the offices occupied. There was a large fitness center with cardio and strength training equipment, and across from that was a massive wine cellar secured behind a glass door. Along the water side was a community kitchen with two commercial stoves, refrigerators, and marble countertops. Lastly, there were two small offices, both with their doors open.

At one desk sat a middle-aged Black woman with close-cropped curly hair. She was dressed in an orange sleeveless athletic polo shirt and a pair of gray athletic dry-wicking cargo shorts. She wasn't paying much attention to us and spun around to grab something off the printer behind her. In the other office was a young man who appeared to be in his twenties. He was busy writing on a whiteboard that was spread out on top of his desk.

"This is Dahlia Stephens," Babs said, gesturing to the woman in the first office. "She's our Fitness and Athletics Manager. She oversees the fitness center, pickleball/tennis courts, and baseball and soccer fields. She has three staff that work for her year-round. If you want a personal trainer, she's your gal, although all her staff are certified."

Dahlia stood up and came around the desk, smiling congenially, and reached out her hand to shake.

"This is Ms. Normand, the new general manager," Babs introduced.

"Please call me Kat," I said. We shook, and then I looked over at the door; the young man had stepped out of his office to introduce himself and extended his hand as well.

"Noah," he said, "Noah Hamelin. I'm the lifestyle manager for the community."

"Lifestyle manager, what exactly does that entail?" I asked politely.

"It's a fancy way of saying that I manage the community activities and events." He shrugged and turned back to his whiteboard. "I've got to get this tournament schedule posted upstairs in the game room lounge; it was a pleasure to meet you. See you later, Babs."

Babs turned back to Dahlia, and the two chatted about last weekend's pickleball tournament. It turned out that Babs was an inveterate pickleball player. Dahlia humored Babs for a little while, then she excused herself, saying she had a personal training session with one of the members. Before she left, she clipped the sheet of paper she had printed onto a clipboard and headed toward the fitness center.

"Well, that's all the folks that work down here. Let's head upstairs so we can wait for Clive."

As we headed back toward the main lounge, we met a short man, only about four and a half feet tall, with short hair and a close-cropped beard. He was bustling about, directing some of the servers and waitstaff.

"Andy! Got a minute?" Babs called.

"Not really, Babs; I've got a brunch booked on the deck for the Lady Lupins, and two of my servers have called out sick today," he said grouchily.

"Well, too bad," Babs said. "This is our new GM. Be nice and shake her hand." She gestured toward me.

"What? When did we get a new GM?" he asked, and robotically extended his hand. I took it and looked quizzically at Babs.

"Don't mind him," she said. "If it doesn't pertain to food, drink, or banquet events, then he doesn't pay any attention to it. A hurricane could blow through here tomorrow, and he wouldn't even notice," she explained.

"That's not fair!" Andy exclaimed. "I'd notice, especially since I would have to ensure that my food didn't spoil when the power went out."

"See what I mean," Babs said, and rolled her eyes.

"I don't have time for your abuse," Andy groaned, and then he took off in the direction of the restaurant. Once again, I felt the urge to scold Babs for teasing the other personnel. However, I again refrained from doing so, as I was still unfamiliar with their interpersonal dynamics.

We took our coffees into the lounge and settled into the big squashy leather armchairs by the unlit fireplace. The sun was coming through the upper window and shone right down to where I was sitting. The air conditioning was on, but the sun was warm, and the chair was comfortable; feeling like I was about to nod off, I pushed myself up abruptly and leaned on the large stone mantle instead.

"Is something wrong?" Babs asked.

"Not at all," I said. "It's just that I didn't sleep well last night, and if I get too comfortable in that chair, I am going to fall asleep and be useless to everyone."

"Yeah, these chairs are quite cozy, and it's nice and quiet in here right now, not too many members buzzing in and out of the building. Lunchtime is when it starts to get busy," Babs explained.

We waited silently for a few minutes, each of us sipping our coffee. I hoped the coffee would give me a much-needed energy boost for the day. It would not do to fall asleep at the helm on my first day of work. Also, it was only ten in the morning, and I still had seven hours of work to get through; it was far too early to start phoning it in just because I hadn't gotten enough sleep the night before.

I looked over in the direction of the main foyer and saw Clive coming into the clubhouse. Once again, he was dressed in a V-neck sweater, collared shirt, and gray slacks that appeared to be made of wool. He must have been sweltering in that outfit; it was already seventy-eight degrees out when I'd walked over just an hour before, and I was sure it had gotten warmer since then. Still, there was not a drop of perspiration on his brow. He smiled at me and pushed his round, wire-rim glasses up on his nose in a habitual gesture. For a second, his tongue flicked out in an almost reptilian way. The odd mannerism startled me a bit, but I assured myself that it was likely just another quirky gesture of his.

"Hi, Clive!" Babs called in a warm greeting. "She's all yours; I've already introduced her to Alice, Dahlia, Noah, and Andy—not that he will remember."

"Leave Andy alone, Babs," Clive scolded. "His single-mindedness is why the restaurant is packed every evening for dinner, and all of our dinner events are sold out for the rest of the year."

"Sold out for the rest of the year?" I was in awe.

"Yep, all the way up to the New Year's Eve black-tie gala. No one in Blackwater Lake misses an event when Andy and Noah coordinate it," Clive said with pride.

"Impressive!" I said.

After Babs excused herself to go back downstairs to the office, Clive suggested that we start with the driving tour, gesturing for me to lead the way out to the front of the building. His car was a black Subaru Impreza. It looked freshly washed, gleaming in the sunlight. He opened the passenger side door for me, and I climbed in. The car couldn't have been parked for more than a few minutes, but the inside was stifling; his air conditioning wasn't on. I shrugged to myself and assumed that he must not have had to drive far.

Clive climbed into the driver's seat and must have noticed my discomfort, because he smiled sheepishly as he turned on the car and switched the climate control from heat to A/C. I couldn't believe he actually had the heat on, but perhaps he had the whole system off and just drove with the windows open. I looked across the car at the dashboard on his side and noticed that all the vents in front of him were closed. The only vent open was the one on the passenger side in front of me. That single vent didn't seem to be doing much to mitigate the heat, so I opted to roll down my windows instead. It was still hot outside, but at least fresh air was circulating. Clive took a cue from me, cut the A/C off, and opened his window too.

"Sorry about that; the A/C doesn't work well in this old thing."

I looked at him, perplexed. The car wasn't new, but it wasn't what you would call old—I would guess four years at most. I doubted that his loan was even paid off, if he had one.

"No problem, I could use the fresh air."

"Well, let me know if you get too uncomfortable. I can try turning the A/C on again, at least for a little while." Clive put the car in gear, pulled out of the roundabout, and headed off to the main road. "Let's go check out Loki Park first. It's one of the closer amenities, except the main waterfront, but we'll save the best for last."

"Sure!" I said. "Sounds like a plan."

CHAPTER SEVEN

Loki Park was charming and had three different-sized playsets: a tot lot, a school-aged play structure, and an advanced ninja course for teens and adults. There was also a basketball court, a splash pad, and a pavilion. We walked the well-shaded path that looped through the whole park and passed a group of moms pushing strollers and talking. Another group of parents sat on the bench under a pergola, watching their young children climb and play a game of imagination.

We paused to watch a group of school-aged kids at the pavilion, who were sitting and listening attentively to a wildlife presentation that featured hands-on demonstrations with snakeskin and deer antlers, as well as a few live wild animal ambassadors. The animals, an opossum, a corn snake, and a turtle, were the stars of the event. The teacher kept reminding the kids that they had to pay attention to the presenter if they wanted the opportunity to pet the critters.

"What school do they go to?" I asked.

"There's a small private school in town; it only serves up to fifth grade. As you can see, they have a very hands-on curriculum," Clive explained.

"Is that the only grade school?" I asked.

"No, that's the private school; it's run by a certain sect," he said.

"A religious school?" I asked.

"No . . . more like a cultural school," Clive offered.

We walked back to the car, and I once again found myself sweltering in the stifling heat of his vehicle. Once the car started moving again and the breeze began to blow through windows, it cooled down a little, but I still regretted my outfit choice. Sure, my clothes were lightweight and linen, but I just knew that they were becoming noticeably damp in certain places. I hoped that the driving tour wouldn't last much longer.

As we drove, I looked at the houses that lined the streets. Each property was different; some appeared to be on quarter-acre lots, and others were much larger. No two houses were alike and appeared to represent a wide array of economic demographics. Some were traditional one-story ranchers or cottage-style lake houses. Others were more colonial in their architecture, with salt-box roofs and gables. Still others were unlike any homes I had ever seen outside of magazines, shaped like geodesic domes and pyramids. The homes that I couldn't really see were the ones that drew my attention the most. Though few in number, the stateliest homes were set back from the road, either down long driveways or hidden behind tall hedgerows. I wondered what the residents of this community were like and looked forward to getting to know more of them.

We toured three beaches on the northeast side of the lake, as well as the north marina. We then went to a second park in the northwest corner of the community. Kataria Park featured twelve pickleball courts, four tennis courts, and a baseball/tee ball field. There were no playgrounds, but it did have a walking trail with some fitness equipment along the path. Despite the heat, every pickleball court had a full foursome playing on it. Although the pickleball players wore sunglasses, caps, and visors to shield their eyes from the sun, no one seemed to be breaking a sweat. They all looked as if they were playing indoors in an air-conditioned gymnasium.

Clive led the way onto the closest court, and as soon as we stepped onto it, the temperature dropped by about twenty degrees. It was comfortable, almost to the point of being too cool to stand around. Still, it would be the perfect temperature for exercise. I looked around to see if we had somehow stepped into a transparent dome, but there was no way to explain the temperature difference. The courts were in the open air, and birds swooped off the fence occasionally to pick at something on the paving. My sweaty, damp clothing started to feel chilly against my skin. I could see that Clive was uncomfortable; he wrapped his arms around himself as if he too was beginning to feel cold. Seeing my confusion, he explained: "It's a climate-controlled court surface."

"I've never heard of such a thing; it must have been expensive. How does it work?" I asked.

"Not sure if I could tell you how it works; it's some new-fangled type of science. One of our members arranged for us to beta-test the product. We're not even sure who manufactured it, but we got it for a song and a dance. The upgrade to the courts was a godsend; it completely negated the need for us to find space for indoor courts during extreme temperatures. These outdoor courts stay the perfect temperature for playing year-round."

I could tell there was probably more to the story than he was letting on, but I decided not to press for details. I would have to see if I could find more information in the board minutes; a project of this scope would certainly have been planned for and approved by the board.

We took our leave of the park and headed for the western side of the community. Clive explained that there weren't many amenities on this end of the neighborhood, mostly just houses and forest. The hilly terrain made it "difficult to build anything of substantial size." As we drove along, I noticed that several of the houses, especially those on the waterfront, were rather large. If a mansion could be built in this area, then I knew we could probably construct some other type of community building over here, but perhaps it was more a problem of there being no available plots of land large enough to accommodate a public building and the parking that would be required.

As we approached the southwest side of the community, a large building the size of two aircraft hangers emerged from the trees, painted a forest green that almost blended in with its surroundings. As we turned into a driveway, I saw that the front of the building featured tall windows that reflected the surrounding tree line, as though the place was designed to be camouflaged with the forest. Clive drove around to the back, where ample parking hid among the trees.

"What purpose does this building serve? It's massive!" I exclaimed.

"This is the Hurston Young Dickenson Recreation Agora," Clive said flatly; it certainly was a mouthful. I paused for a second to decode the acronym in my head.

"Wait, HYDRA? You named your community center HYDRA?!" I asked incredulously.

"Well, no, not really. We call it The Agora. It was named after the first community volunteer who started all recreational activities in the 1960s. He was amazing! According to our archives, he could coach and play tennis, water skiing, and coach and play basketball. Legend has it that he was once a Harlem Globetrotter. He was an all-around good guy, and everyone loved spending time with him. When we built this building nearly ten years ago, the board decided it would be best to name it in honor of him," Clive explained. "Why don't I give you a tour? Come on inside."

We walked into the building and out of the heat. I was grateful for the air conditioning. The large front windows lit the space beautifully; the sun shone through the trees and caused the shadows of the trees to dapple the floor. A grand fountain with benches sat prominently in the center of the massive foyer. To the right was an administrative desk where two young staffers sat clacking away at computers. To the left was a wall of benches, an elevator, and a series of digital screens that showed the schedule for each room in the building, ads for upcoming events and activities, and notices of meetings. Two corridors stretched off to each side of the foyer, and just beyond the fountain was a wide, sweeping staircase that led up to a landing with a set of double doors at the top; the stairs continued to either side of the doorway, leading up to the second floor. Lettering above the doors read "P. Jackson Hall."

"P. Jackson was the first board president," said Clive, following my gaze. "No one really knows what his first name was. He normally just went by Jackson, but he would sign all his letters, P. Jackson. The hall is where we hold board meetings, town halls, presentations, and such."

We walked into the hall, and above our heads was a balcony with two permanently mounted cameras. There was an A/V control computer and a mixing board. The theater-style seating spread out on either side of an aisle and sloped down to a dais with nine seats, each with built-in microphones and a small digital display angled so that board members could easily follow along with PowerPoint presentations or the agenda. It was an incredibly sophisticated set-up for an HOA. The extravagance of this community continued to astound me.

"This is amazing!" I exclaimed.

"You will be seated in the chair at the end of the table, stage right," Clive explained. "We have board meetings once a month, and they are usually well attended. Amy and Tyler, the two staff people that were up front, run the A/V system during the meetings."

"Wow, what goes on in the rest of the building?" I asked.

"C'mon, I'll show you." He gestured, and we walked back out toward the foyer. The ground floor consisted of an indoor pool housed in one wing and a gymnasium in the other. Each wing had its own set of locker rooms.

The gym could double as a theatre, with panels for a stage set into the wall that could be pulled out like a giant Murphy bed and set up for use. The long walls of the gym also had recessed telescopic bleachers that could be pulled out to form four banks of seating with an aisle down the middle. The system was practically invisible, and if Clive hadn't pointed it out, then I wouldn't have even known it was there. Across from the main entrance to the gym was another pair of double doors, which Clive said led to a storage room.

The second floor had a game room, craft room, and four classroom spaces. The classrooms were well stocked and organized; each had access to a closet, and each wing had a pair of bathrooms. This was the most fantastic community center that I had ever seen. It was like a combination of a YMCA and a college campus community building. It was well lit and welcoming. The floors were vinyl tile but had the look of polished marble, with streaks of warm hardwood bracketing each side of the corridor. This building must have cost millions to build, and given the rural nature of the community, I was hard-pressed to see how they could have raised the capital to construct it. When had Clive said this place was built? Almost ten years ago? If that was true, I realized, then it must have been constructed within the first five years of Odeon's career here as manager.

"This must have been a massive project; I'm guessing the planning process started well before Odeon became the general manager. Surely, he had to hit the ground running to bring a project like this to fruition so soon after he started working here."

Clive raised an eyebrow and peered at me through his wire-rim glasses. We were back down in the foyer, and I was sitting on the edge of the fountain; Clive was standing a few feet away from me in one of the brighter, sunnier spots, looking almost like a lizard sunning itself on a rock.

"Yes, I imagine he must have; I wasn't living here at that time. I've only lived here about five years myself. But from what I've heard, there was a great deal of community support for this project. The Friends of Blackwater Lake Foundation, our non-profit arm, raised most of the money. The bulk of the donations came from legacy family members, often children of residents who grew up here and moved away."

"Still, it's quite a remarkable place for an HOA," I said.

We hung out in the foyer in silence for a few more minutes. I would have been happy to sit there for another half hour listening to the fountain and enjoying the air conditioning, but Clive wanted to continue with the driving tour. We hopped back into his car, and the moment I sat down, I felt myself melting. If I stayed in his car much longer, I would need an IV to rehydrate.

But the tour didn't take much longer. We drove past several amenities without stopping, including an equestrian center, two more parks—one featuring a large outdoor pool—and three beaches. When we pulled into the parking lot at South Beach, I looked around, trying to imagine what Willow had seen. She had come upon Odeon's empty car here, still running with the driver's side door open. The beach was not empty now, two families sat under the shade of one of the pergolas and young children played in the water. Now was probably my best opportunity to ask Clive what he knew about Odeon's disappearance. We were still in his car, so I knew that the two families wouldn't hear me ask this sensitive question.

"Clive, why didn't anybody tell me what happened to Arthur Odeon? I had to hear about it from the town's chief of police. I feel like that was important information that I needed when I was deciding whether or not to work here." I knew my tone was accusatory, but it was difficult for me not to feel like I had been slighted.

"I had a feeling that you had heard the story, especially when you asked about Odeon back at the Community Center. So, it was the chief that you heard it from? Figures," Clive said, not answering my question. I gestured for him to go on. "The other board members and I were worried that you wouldn't have come if you knew about it before accepting the job. It was already strange enough that we were asking you to work out here in such a remote location. We needed a qualified manager and didn't want to take the chance that you would say no," he explained.

"That's a little bit shifty. None of my research, or my friend's, yielded any useful information about this place; I was entirely dependent on what you and Babs were telling me. You should have said something about this." I crossed my arms and glared at him.

"I'm sorry, you're right. I wanted to tell you sooner, before we sent the moving truck for your belongings, but I was outvoted."

I stared at the lake momentarily, wishing that I could just take a dive and go for a swim. The sweat on my brow was dripping into my eyes, and my linen clothes were plastered to me in an unflattering way. Plus, the frustration and anger that I felt about having this information concealed from me was ramping up my temper, and my temperature, further contributing to my discomfort.

"What happened to Odeon? Do I have anything to be worried about?" I finally asked.

"We don't know what happened. He just disappeared one night after our annual meeting. I'm sure you've heard the details: Willow found his car here at this beach, parked right over there. The engine was still running, and the door was wide open. The inside of the car was wet because it had rained that night. The beach had been washed clear of footprints due to the rain. There was no other sign of him. I personally think it was suicide. He had not really been himself of late, and he had been acting very strangely. I had to take him aside and talk to him about his work attendance. He would disappear in the middle of the day, sometimes even when he had prior commitments. Such a change in personality makes me certain that he was depressed and dealing with some mental health issues."

"Did you try to get him help?" I asked. "It seems like he needed it. He was giving all indications that there was a problem."

"We did. Vinny, one of our longest-serving board members, took him aside; he was closest to Arthur, and they sometimes hung out together. He reminded him of our benefits package, which includes an employee assistance program with a mental health hotline. We offered to give him some extra time off if he needed it. Babs and I could hold down the fort if he needed to take some leave. But he waved Vinny off, saying that he didn't need any help; he was doing just fine. What could we do? We had to take his word for it."

I could tell I had struck a nerve, and I apologized for pointing the blame at him and the other board members. It wasn't their fault. Clive was right, you could offer people help, but they had to be willing to accept it. I took one more look around the beach; I still wasn't sold on the idea of suicide. How could he have done such a thing from this beach? Even if he swam out into the lake until he ran out of energy and strength, his body would have likely shown up by now.

I thought about a news article I had read about a month ago. A young mother in Maryland had attempted suicide by drowning. She had been suffering from postpartum depression and drove her car into the large retention pond near her home. Once she got into the water, she panicked and tried to escape, but the car doors would not unlock. The system was shorted out by the water. Luckily for her, an off-duty firefighter lived right next door. He had been doing the dishes and watched her car roll into the water. He ran out his back door, grabbed an axe from his firewood pile, hurried into the water, smashed the window, and extracted her from the car. How much more willpower would it have taken to swim out beyond the point of no return? With that macabre thought in my mind, Clive started up his Dutch oven of a car, and we set off toward the clubhouse again.

"Well, I've saved the best for last. We'll head back, check out the clubhouse's waterfront, and then get lunch on the deck of the Roanoke," he said, forcing himself to sound cheerful.

"Um, thanks for the offer for lunch, but could we eat inside instead of on the deck? This heat is really getting to me, and I wouldn't mind being in the air conditioning for a while."

Clive shivered almost imperceptibly, as if the very idea of air conditioning was enough to give him a chill. What was up with the guy? Was he dealing with some sort of medical issue? I would have to keep a closer eye on him to ensure he was okay.

"Sure," he said. "I'm afraid I will have to take my leave anyway, but the other board members wanted to join you for lunch. You haven't yet had a chance to meet Vinny, Felix, Rose, and Michael. I'll introduce you when we arrive, but I will have to head out; I promised my granddaughter I would meet her at the school bus after kindergarten." He sounded a little more like himself.

We headed back to the clubhouse and walked around the beach. On the opposite end of the building from the offices, below the panoramic deck on the main floor, was an open-air work counter, behind which hung three rows of lifejackets displayed on three horizontal poles. A black and white letterboard featured the prices for canoe, kayak, sailboat, and stand-up paddleboard rentals. A whiteboard showed the schedule of lessons and events on the lake. Apparently, a full moon paddle was scheduled for midnight on Saturday, and sure enough, there was a kayak lesson scheduled for this afternoon with "Instructor Babs."

A middle-aged man with a deep tan, sun-bleached blond hair, and a swimmer's build came around the corner of the building with a stand-up paddleboard under his arm. He was dressed in a bright orange polo shirt and black swim trunks. He propped the paddleboard into the rack and then turned to greet us, beaming brightly.

"What's SUP!" he asked and burst out laughing. When we didn't join him, he said, "Get it, *SUP*? As in stand-up paddleboard?"

I smiled and laughed awkwardly. It was a corny joke, but I liked his vibrant style. He was easy to warm up to and immediately gave me the impression that he was confident and competent at what he did.

"Kat, this is Donny Roget, the waterfront manager. He manages the marina, the watercraft rentals, and lake activities. As you may have guessed, his favorite activity is stand-up paddleboard. He even teaches SUP Yoga," Clive said by way of introduction. I tried to picture what that would look like, but I couldn't.

"What exactly is SUP Yoga?" I asked.

"I have a gear-shaped instructor raft that I anchor out in the cove, just off the main beach. It can have up to eight paddleboards docked to it, forming a star shape on the water. My ladies paddle out, tie up, and spend about an hour doing yoga with me. It's so popular that I have one class every morning throughout the summer and a little bit into the fall," Donny explained. I could just imagine the women of the neighborhood swooning over him, with his bright smile, charming personality, and good looks. However, I had an inkling that Donny was off the market, for women at least.

"Congratulations. Can you get me a spot in a class someday?" I asked, hoping that the answer would be no. I wasn't a morning person, and yoga at seven a.m. on the lake sounded like a chore.

"You're in luck! I just had a cancellation this morning. Brianne has to get surgery this week and will be out of commission for about a month. You can take her spot and try it out! The class is on Mondays at seven a.m."

I cringed inwardly but plastered on a smile.

"Great! I look forward to it; see you later." And I filed away that new commitment for later.

Clive and I walked off toward the beach, which featured a large sandy area perfect for families to enjoy lake life activities such as building sandcastles and playing in the water. A picnic grove with a fishing dock, gazebo, and a small playground was set off to the side. The bright blue sky reflected off the water and made the lake appear a bright azure blue. In the distance, the hills at the far end embraced the landscape as if they were hugging the whole community.

"This really is a beautiful place," I told Clive. "Thank you for the opportunity to be the manager here. I didn't mean to come off as ungrateful earlier; it's just that this whole situation with Odeon has me feeling a bit uneasy. The fact that it's a mystery that hasn't been solved is even more unsettling. I feel like I should be doing something about it, not just driving around having a guided tour of the community."

"There is nothing for you to do; the chief and Detective Daniels have it covered. It's a law enforcement matter, not an HOA matter."

I wanted to disagree, but I couldn't find a valid argument to make my point.

Clive looked at his watch and then grinned at me.

"Lunch time! Let's go meet the rest of the board members."

I slipped my phone out of my pocket and looked at the clock. Sure enough, it was about a quarter to noon. I hadn't realized that two hours had passed while we were out on our tour. I was sure that I hadn't seen everything. This place was just too big. I felt another knot adding itself to the jumble in my stomach. The feeling of inadequacy and doubt crept back into my mind. I wasn't sure if I was prepared to manage a community of this size on my own without a management firm backing me. Maybe that's why I kept trying to dive into the mystery of the disappearing GM. I was almost less intimidated by the idea of solving a missing person case than I was about taking on this new role. I shrugged off these feelings and gestured for Clive to lead the way to lunch.

CHAPTER EIGHT

Lunch passed uneventfully. I had hoped to learn a bit more about the history of the association, but it was a typical meet-and-greet filled with small talk and platitudes. Clive made the introductions and then, as promised, left to meet his granddaughter at the school bus stop. Any time one of the board members tried to bring up business, Hilary would smile and remind them that they had promised not to bore me with the details on my first day.

Lunch was delicious. I ordered a balsamic chicken and roasted vegetable wrap that was served with roasted baby potatoes. Even though I had guzzled down a glass of ice water, I was still very parched, so I ordered lightly sweetened raspberry iced tea with my meal. It was a light meal, but surprisingly filling given the anxiety taking up much of the room in my stomach.

Afterward, I hoped to meet up with Babs back in the office, but she had already taken off to teach the kayak lesson. She left a note for me on her desk telling me that she would be back by two p.m. and that she had left some binders containing the governing documents on the table in my office. I figured that was as good a task as any right now, and I was grateful to have some quiet time in my own office and to be in the air conditioning. My clothes had dried while we were at lunch and I had cooled back down considerably, but the heat had taken a lot out of me.

I grabbed a plastic cup from the dispenser and filled it with water from the cooler. It was ice cold and refreshing; I drank it down in one long gulp, refilled the cup, and headed back to my office, making a mental note to bring a water bottle with me tomorrow.

I stepped into my office and saw the set of five three-inch-thick binders standing upright on my conference table. I decided to spend some time reading through them to familiarize myself with the rules and regulations of this place. It was my job after all, and I couldn't always count on Babs to get me the answer. I stood there a moment, staring at the books as if I could absorb all the information by osmosis. Well, there was nothing for it; I needed to get to work.

As I pulled out a chair at the conference table, I noticed that there was a little piece of paper wedged in between the leather cushion and the arm of the chair. I was sure that the office had been cleaned since Odeon's disappearance, but a little piece of paper like this would have been easy to miss. I picked it up and headed over to the desk to find the trash can, but as I did, I saw that there was writing on it.

I took a seat at my desk to see if I could make out the scribbled handwriting. The piece of paper in my hand read "*outh beach.*" Then I noticed that the desk blotter pad had a corner torn off and the piece in my hand looked like it could belong there, I tried to fit the piece back into the corner. The paper fit, but there was still a good portion of the note that was missing and I couldn't complete the message. Even without the rest of the message, I could easily conclude that it was supposed to say, "South Beach."

Well, that seems too coincidental, I thought.

I was certain that this note had something to do with the case. Perhaps Odeon had written this down before he had disappeared. I wondered what happened to the rest of the note. I looked down into the trash can, but it had been recently emptied and had a fresh plastic bag liner. It had been months since Arthur Odeon had disappeared, I was sure that if the rest of the note had been thrown away, then it was long gone by now.

I opened some of the drawers in the desk to see if I could find any other clues. Strangely, I felt a bit guilty, as if I was snooping, even though it *was* my desk. I didn't see anything out of place. Just some paper clips, a stapler, a roll of scotch tape, pens, sticky notes, and a pencil.

A pencil?

A thought occurred to me just then. When I was just fourteen and my older brother was seventeen, he had started dating a girl from school. Like many a teenaged boy in the '90s, he would spend hours sitting at our counter and talking to her on the phone after school while our dad was still at work. They never actually said much of anything, just a bunch of cooing and fawning over each other, but occasionally he would write something down on the note pad on the counter.

One Friday night, he had gone out on a date with her and didn't tell my dad where he was going. Once my father got home from work, he paced back and forth in the kitchen for about an hour.

Nowadays, he would have texted my brother or called his cellphone, but it was 1994 and those methods of communication weren't an option yet.

It was only seven at night, which wasn't that late, but my dad was worried because he had no idea where my brother had gone—he hadn't left a note or told me to relay any messages. By about seven thirty, my dad had his truck keys in his hand and was just about to go out and drive around town to look for him, when I remembered that I had seen my brother write a note on the phone message pad before he left. I ran over to the counter; sure enough, I could see the impression of the note still etched into the blank sheet behind it. I took a pencil from the jar on the counter and shaded over the marks to reveal what my brother had written: *Waynes World 2- 5:30, Pizza Hut.* I showed my father the note, and he tossed his keys into the basket on the counter and threw himself down at the kitchen table. My brother finally came home around eight o'clock and by then, I had made myself scarce up in my bedroom. It didn't matter though; I easily heard the scolding that he got from our father about his lack of communication.

Taking inspiration from this memory, I plucked the pencil out of the drawer and began a gentle frottage over the paper. I was careful not to press too hard or the pressure would erase any trace of a message. Slowly the message began to reveal itself, but it wasn't the groundbreaking, case solving note that I had been hoping for. In fact, it was pretty much nonsense:

Go to south beach and follow the bird.
Follow the bird go to south beach.
Go to south beach follow the bird.
Follow the bird go to south beach.

I didn't know what to make of it, but it was apparent that Arty Odeon had been losing his mind right before he disappeared. I sat down at his desk, or rather my desk, and looked around to see if there were any other clues. Indeed, on closer inspection I realized there were drawings of birds on almost every piece of paper on the desk. They were little more than doodles, the type of bird that looked like an elongated letter *M*, and they would certainly have been easy to overlook or be disregarded by the police. However, the note that I had uncovered hinted that the doodles might have a deeper meaning.

I was debating what to do next when Babs bustled in through the door. She had a towel wrapped around her shoulders and was dripping with sweat. For some reason, she had kept her flannel shirt on over her tank top, even though it was obvious that she was melting from the heat.

"Hi there, how was the tour?" she said brightly.

"The tour?" I asked, distracted.

"Yeah, with Clive. Didn't he take you on a tour of the community? I thought that was the plan."

"Oh, yes, of course. It was great, the neighborhood is beautiful. I especially liked the community center, although I'm a little . . . um, shocked isn't quite the right word . . . maybe mystified, that the center is called HYDRA. Isn't that the bad guy group in all the Marvel movies?"

"Well, it was the bad guy monster in the Hercules legend long before Marvel appropriated it. But we don't call it HYDRA anyway, we just call it the Agora, which is an ancient Greek community gathering place." She took a long look at me. The stress of today's events must have shown on my face.

"What's up with you?" she asked. "How are you settling in? You seem a little upset."

I beckoned her over and showed her what I had found on the desk blotter, both the words and all the drawings of birds.

"Hmmm, I never noticed that before, and I've been in this office a dozen times since Arty disappeared. I needed to get it organized and prepared for our new GM." She glanced around the office and looked at the artwork. Following suit, I noticed there were birds everywhere. They were in the some of the smaller prints on the wall, in the etchings on the door, and there were even some figurines on his shelf.

"I think I am detecting a trend here; how did I not notice all of the bird motifs in this office?" Babs said in surprise.

"I think we should call the police and ask them to send someone. Do you know the non-emergency number?"

"Oh, I'll just text Jay and he'll probably send Detective Dingleberry over here," Babs said, casually whipping her phone out of her pocket.

"Wait, what?" I wasn't sure if I was more thrown off by the fact that she had the chief's cellphone number and called him by his first name, or the fact that she had used the words *Detective Dingleberry.*

"I have Jay's cell number—comes in handy when things go sideways in the community. Arty used to ask me to contact Jay all the time for different HOA issues." She swiped her finger around on her phone screen to type out a message.

"Who is Detective Dingleberry?" I prompted.

"Detective Daniels. He's not the freshest peach in the peck," she griped.

"He must be somewhat smart. He did make the rank of detective, after all," I argued.

"No, he must have an uncle who's the mayor of the town—or *was* the mayor of the town. There was a turnover last November and Dingleberry's uncle was voted out. The only reason that he is still on the force is because there haven't been any real cases for him to screw up. However, this missing person case sure is a good contender. I think Chief may be looking for a reason to fire him soon," she said, as her phone chirped. "The chief is on his way here himself. I guess we are spared the presence of the Dink."

Babs sat down in one of the chairs across from my desk, and we chatted about office topics for about fifteen minutes until the chief arrived. While we waited, we both continued to inspect the office, trying to interpret the themes of the artwork that surrounded us. It was clear that the artwork had something to do with Greek mythology, one even featured a weathered map of the Aegean Sea and the archipelago islands. I wondered if Arty's note was perhaps related to the legend of the albatross. Perhaps he felt as if he had done something to inflict a curse or bad omen upon the HOA. I stared at a shelf of bird statues, as they had the most detail. But the birds didn't look like albatrosses to me; they weren't fully white, but rather were chestnut brown with white chests and heads. I was at a loss for what type of bird they could have been.

When the chief arrived, I explained what I had discovered. I tried to keep any speculation out of my story, but I did mention my albatross idea.

"I don't think these birds are albatrosses," the chief said as he studied a photo of a bird on the hutch above the desk. "I actually think they might be ospreys."

"Does that mean anything special?" I asked.

"Not that I can think of," he said, and then turned toward the door of the office, which had been left slightly ajar. As if on cue, the door opened fully, and a tall woman stepped into the room. Her blond hair was so fine it was almost iridescent. With her almond shaped eyes and heart-shaped lips highly done up with makeup, she looked like a model or an Instagram influencer.

"Honey, do you recall anything significant about ospreys?" the chief asked her.

Honey? I thought, and I felt my stomach lurch.

"No. Are you going to be much longer?" she asked, looking impatient.

"Not much longer; why don't you head upstairs to The Roanoke and order yourself a glass of wine. I'll be up in a little while."

"Oh sure, go ahead, don't mind us furniture here in the office!" Babs protested.

Jay looked at Babs, confused, but then realized his faux pas.

"Sorry, I should have made introductions. Jessica, this is our new general manager, Katherine Normand; Kat, this is my fiancé, Jessica Cheverie. And Babs, I think you know Jessica already," he said, and gave Babs the side-eye.

"Yeah, I know her. How'ya doin' Jess?" Babs said, and gave her a salute.

"It's Jessica, Barbara, and I would be much better if I were up-stairs at the bar with a glass of Prosecco," Jessica complained.

"Well don't let us keep ya," Babs said bluntly.

"Jay, when you are done playing art critic, come find me. I'll be upstairs talking with Keyana," she said, then turned on her kitten heels and strutted out the door.

An awkward and heavy silence descended on the room. I was not quite sure what to say or do. Fortunately, Babs seemed to have no such compunctions.

"She was a delight as always, Jay. Why did you bring her along?" she said, asking the question that was on my mind as well.

"I'm technically off the clock right now. I left work a little early and we were coming over here for dinner when I got your text. I figured I would check everything out before I called in Detective Daniels. Speaking of whom, he's on his way over. Can I ask you two to leave the office so he and our forensic tech can check this place over again for any other evidence?"

"Sure . . ." I said in exasperation. *I mean it's not like it's my office yet, anyway. I've barely spent an hour in the place,* I thought.

"It's just for the afternoon, I promise. We've already looked the place over previously, but we want to go over everything one more time to see if there was anything else that we might have missed," Jay said, accurately reading my expression.

"Why don't you head on home with these?" Babs said, and scooped an armload of binders off the conference table. "You can get started on reading them. There's nothing you can really do here in the office until Ned from IT gets you up and running tomorrow."

"I don't know about that, there could be evidence in there," Jay said, reaching for the binders.

"Don't be an idiot. These are from *my office*, there's no evidence in them," Babs said, dodging his reach. "C'mon Kat, I have a tote bag you can borrow to carry this home."

I followed Babs back out into the main office area, and she found a canvas tote bag in the bottom drawer of her desk. She unceremoniously stuck the five binders into the tote, then hefted the straps onto my shoulder.

"Should I let Clive know that I'm heading home early?" I asked, not really knowing what the etiquette was for such things.

"Nope. You keep your own schedule. Just don't go AWOL like Arty did and you'll be fine," she said, and gave me a shove toward the staircase.

"Okay . . ." I said, hesitantly. "I guess I'll see you tomorrow morning then. Call or text me if anything comes up."

"Nothing will *come up*," Babs said as she sat back down at her desk. She once again picked up her copy of *The Art of Managing Up*.

Feeling as if I was being dismissed by my own executive assistant, and frustrated that my office had turned into a crime scene, I trudged up the stairs with my heavy bag of binders. I made another mental note that in addition to a water bottle, I would have to find a good quality backpack or messenger bag to carry things to and from work. I had a feeling that this wouldn't be the last time that I brought work home with me.

By the time I got back to the house, my clothes were sticking to me again; my blouse, especially, felt like it was becoming transparent. Thankfully there wasn't anyone else around.

As I reached into the pocket of my purse, which I had stashed in the tote bag, to fish out the house key, I sensed that I was being watched. I looked up. On one of the Adirondack chairs on the porch sat Jet, the springer spaniel. He was sitting like a perfect gentleman, with his two front paws crossed over each other. He looked so adorable, but he also looked like trouble. There was a glint in his eyes that made me suspect the dog was up to something.

"To what do I owe the pleasure?" I asked with a tone of formality, and attempted to bow to him. I nearly fell over on my face, as laden as I was with my belongings. The dog didn't answer, of course, but he perked up his fluffy ears and looked at me quizzically.

"Well, I guess you better come on in and cool off," I said, and with some careful maneuvering, managed to get the door open. The dog hopped down off the chair and followed me inside. He brushed past my legs and headed into the main living area.

I followed him inside, went over to the kitchen island, and dropped my tote bag on the counter. I looked around the house and tried to decide where I wanted to sit and read, finally deciding that it would be worth lugging the heavy binders up to the lounge area on the second floor, if only so that I could enjoy the view of the lake from time to time. I was not looking forward to the stack of boring documents that I had to read.

Before I headed upstairs, I filled a bowl of water for Jet and grabbed a can of strawberry-watermelon sparkling water from the refrigerator for myself. Jet moseyed over and slowly lapped up the water as I popped open the can of sparkling water, tilted it back, and drank it down in just a couple of swallows. I let out a loud belch, so loud that Jet jumped back and looked at me, dumbfounded.

"Whoops, glad no one was here to see that!" I reached into the refrigerator for another can.

I was still thirsty from spending so much time in the heat. I probably could have finished this can off in a hurry as well, but I decided that it would be best to take my time. I held off on opening it until I got upstairs so it wouldn't spill while I lugged the tote bag of binders up to the second floor.

When I got upstairs, I first changed out of my sweaty, damp clothes, dropping the tote bag near one of the comfy basket chairs that overlooked the lower living space as I trudged into my bedroom, stripped down, and threw my clothing down the laundry chute I'd found in my closet that morning. I grabbed my yoga pants and T-shirt off the foot of my bed and threw them on. Between the dry, comfortable clothes and the air conditioning, I was already feeling much more human than the slimy slug-person that I had been a few minutes ago.

I came out of my room and found Jet curled up on the floor next to my chair. I was impressed to see that for once, the pup wasn't sitting on the furniture, yet I felt another pang of worry as I wondered what to do with him. I needed to find out who Jet belonged to.

I reached down into the tote bag for my phone and pulled up my text thread with Babs, then took a quick photo of Jet and sent her a message that read *Guess who is visiting my house again?*

Babs texted me right back: *That gosh darn dog! Tell him that he won't be allowed to go to the concert on Friday if he doesn't go home.*

"The concert?" I asked aloud, looking down at Jet. His ears perked up, as if he'd understood me.

"Well, Jet, Babs says that if you don't go home, then you won't be allowed to go to the concert on Friday . . . whatever that means."

Jet, however, seemed to know exactly what it meant. He jumped up and ran downstairs to the back door. I followed along as quickly as I could to let him out of the house, and Jet scurried off as fast as his little feet could take him. He didn't even glance back at me.

"Bye!" I shouted, then realized that I still didn't know where his home was. I would have to remember to ask Babs tomorrow. I didn't like the idea that the dog was walking around the neighborhood and along the twisty, narrow roads and running the risk of getting hit.

I turned back and headed upstairs, got comfortable in the chair, and took a long swig of sparkling water. I was procrastinating and I knew it. I looked down at the spines of the binders to see which one I wanted to crack open first.

The spines read:

Plat, Declaration of Restrictions, Articles of Incorporation
Bylaws
Rules & Regulations
Resolutions
Minutes

"Well, that there is some exciting reading," I muttered to myself.

I decided to start with the minutes. I hoped to get a better understanding of the most recent priorities for the association.

At first it was dull reading, and I fought to keep myself awake. The minutes for May, June, and July were boring and read like any other association's minutes. There was a call to order, and a summary of the member comments; then brief descriptions of the motions that were made during new business and unfinished business. The motions and action items in the more recent sets of minutes were straightforward. There was a motion to replace the diving board at the pool, an administrative resolution to move funds from one account to another, and a discussion of maintenance contracts, just to name a few. I was feeling buoyed by the minutes. Sure, they were boring, but familiarity with them meant that I would be able to get up to speed faster. That confidence faded when I reached the minutes from April.

They were barely written in English. While some of the words were recognizable, the rest was more like gibberish. I skimmed ahead in mounting panic. Every few pages there appeared to be a musical score that someone had handwritten in the margins. None of it made any sense. I rapidly flipped through the pages, trying to see how far back the damage went. It was only when I got to the October minutes that they returned to normalcy.

I checked each set of minutes to see who had written them. The minutes between November and April appeared to be written by Arthur Odeon himself and weren't signed off by the board secretary, Hilary Wen. While it was not uncommon, it was not typically considered good etiquette to have the general manager take the minutes. The minutes that were taken prior to November and after April were scribed by a woman named Margery Belle. Hilary Wen still appeared to be the secretary who signed off on them.

"What the heck!" I exclaimed. "Did the board just not see six months' worth of minutes, or did Arty somehow replace them with nonsense?" I asked myself aloud.

I tried to make some sense of it all but to no avail. However, I began to see a pattern, and a timeline began to click into place in my head. About a year and a half ago, Arthur Odeon divorced his wife; then he became quiet for about six months. He kept mostly to himself and plugged along at his job without cause for concern. Then, in November of last year, Odeon had started to spiral into madness. He spent less and less time at work and often went AWOL and spent a great deal of time on the lake.

Around that same time, he started to invest his own money into redecorating his office with an elaborate sailing ship and ancient Greek motif. He also took over responsibility for keeping the meeting minutes from the scribe, and his writing grew progressively less and less coherent. All of this occurred in the months leading up to his disappearance on the night of May first.

Six months. The community, his friends, his boss . . . they had six months to intervene. Clive had said that they tried to offer him assistance and he'd shrugged it off, but surely there must have been something more they could have done. All the signs of distress were there *before* he disappeared. The timeline indicated that around last October, there must have been some sort of event that triggered this behavior. I would have to talk to Babs and do a little more research to find out what might have happened.

I tossed the minutes binder back into my tote bag, sighed deeply, then blindly reached back in and pulled out the first binder that I touched. It was the *Rules & Regulations* binder.

Guess, I'm starting here, I thought to myself. *Hope these aren't as crazy as the minutes were.* I flipped the binder open to the first page and started reading some perfectly boring, perfectly normal rules and regulations.

CHAPTER NINE

In the morning, I headed back to work with a water bottle in one hand and the tote bag over my shoulder. I was dressed in a slightly more practical pair of khaki capris, a sleeveless blouse, and my pair of comfy, everyday ballet flats. My golden-brown hair was pulled up off the nape of my neck and into a clip. The nest of anxiety knots had not fully untangled themselves, but I felt a little better. I had slept well, lulled to sleep by reading the association's rules and regulations. I found myself with much more energy than I had the previous day. To top it off, there was no springer spaniel sitting on my front porch waiting for me. I had the distinct feeling that today was going to be a better day.

However, as I walked up to the clubhouse and around to the back, I heard the jingle of dog tags and the huff of happy panting. I spun around and saw Jet prancing along behind me; his tail wagged, and his tongue lolled out. He yipped once at me in greeting.

"Well hello to you, too," I said, and smiled down at him. "Are you supposed to be here? I'm sure that I read about a regulation that dogs must always be on a leash."

Jet tilted his head at me. The gesture seemed to suggest that he understood what I was saying, but he wasn't sure the rules applied to him.

"C'mon, then," I said. "Babs will know what to do with you . . . again." He didn't seem phased by this remark, he just trotted along ahead of me toward the door to the offices.

Babs hadn't had a chance yet to give me a set of keys to the office, so I was banking on the idea that she was a morning person and was probably already there. My gamble paid off, and sure enough she was already at work typing away at her computer. *The Art of Managing Up* sat coverside-up on her desk. I got the impression that she was trying to send me a message. I strategically ignored it and pressed on as if the book wasn't even there.

"Good morning, look who found me outside."

Babs glanced up and then stood up, placing hands on her desk so that she could peer down at the chipper springer spaniel, who was happily thumping his tail on the floor.

"Jet," she said scoldingly. "Don't you have somewhere to be?"

Jet just tilted his head in his stubborn but lovable way.

"You can get going, or I can call Mr. Worthman."

With that admonition, Jet turned on his heels and headed to the door. I pushed it open for him and he took off at a sprint, back up the embankment and around to the front of the clubhouse.

"Who's Mr. Worthman?" I asked.

"He's the Principal at the middle school," Babs replied bluntly.

"Oh, is that who Jet belongs to?" I asked.

"Only during the school day," Babs responded.

I once again wondered why Babs was being so evasive about telling me who Jet belonged to. Every time I asked her, she seemed to come up with some new way to avoid fully answering the question. It was getting irksome.

"How was your evening? Did you get much reading done?" she asked. I shook myself from my thoughts and brought myself back to the conversation.

"Somewhat. I made it through the bylaws and about half of the rules and regulations. I'll have to get caught up today."

She waved off my concerns. "Nah, you'll have plenty of time to figure it out as you go. Our IT guy is going to be here soon, and he will get you set up on your computer and help you configure your phone."

"Thanks; can you please let me into my office? I still don't have a set of keys yet."

"Willow dropped off a set for you this morning. She put them on your desk. They are all labeled, so you should be able to find what you need pretty quickly. Your office is already unlocked," Babs explained.

"Excellent, well, I guess I'll get settled in while I wait for the IT guy. What was his name again?"

"Ned, Ned Dennys."

"Ned Dennys?" I asked, thinking that it was such an unfortunate name. I could only imagine what type of mischief his school mates came up with when he was a kid.

"Yeah, sometimes I like to call him Den," Babs said.

"Does he like to be called Den?" I asked, incredulous. Babs just shrugged in response, which led me to think she had made up another nickname. I would have to do something about her predilection to call people by something other than their preferred name. I shook my head and turned to my office. The elaborate etched artwork on the door reminded me of something that Babs had said recently.

"Hey Babs, didn't you say that Odeon's ex-wife was into birds?"

"Yeah, why?" she asked.

"It's just . . . well, I wonder if that has anything to do with why there are birds decorating his office. Maybe he was hoping to get back with his ex?" I guessed.

"Nah, I doubt it, but I guess if you really wanted to know then you could ask Jess."

"Jessica? The chief's fiancé?" I asked, puzzled.

"Yep, she's best friends with Arty's ex-wife. I think they still keep in touch with each other."

"I guess that kind of fits, from what I know about both of them, as little as that is."

There was still something scratching at the back of my mind that made me want to connect Odeon's ex with his disappearance, but I would have to dig into that some other time. I hefted the tote bag back up onto my shoulder and then remembered the minutes.

"Hey Babs, have you looked at the minutes, the ones from November through May, right up until Mr. Odeon disappeared?" I asked her.

"No, I can't say I have," she said.

"I find that hard to believe," I said. "Surely, there was some vote or action that you needed to look back and verify. The motions at the meetings determine the business of the association."

"But you forget, Arty was still here then. He may have been slowly riding the crazy train, but he was still in charge. I didn't have any reason to look at the minutes at that time. Why do you ask?" she said, and crossed her arms.

"Because they are complete nonsense. There's nothing in them but gibberish, and they are not signed off by the secretary, Hilary Wen. I'm sure she must have asked to see them. In fact, I'm sure the whole board would have seen them before they voted to approve them at the next meeting. How on earth could such obvious garbage have been approved by the board?"

"Nonsense? That's impossible," Babs said. I pulled out the binder to show her, flipping to the January minutes.

"See," I said, pointing to the first page.

"What? What am I supposed to be looking at?" she asked.

I looked down at the page and instead of the gibberish that had been there before, the minutes were well written and properly formatted. It was as if they were written by the author of Robert's Rules himself.

"That makes no sense," I muttered, and flipped between the minutes from November to May. Each month was perfect, and nothing seemed out of place. They were all signed and approved by "Hilary Wen, Secretary." Babs looked at me, concerned, and stuck her hands into the pockets of her denim shirt dress in a motherly way that I didn't very much care for.

"Are you sure you got enough sleep last night?" she asked. "You didn't try and read all of those documents at once, did you? It's not a test, you know, you don't have to cram."

"Yes, I got enough sleep, and I'm certain of what I saw yesterday. I know that the minutes weren't there. It was just a bunch of gibberish!" I said defensively.

"What was gibberish?" a male voice asked behind me.

I spun around and saw a tall man with glasses and a well-groomed beard. He was young, probably thirty or so, but the beard made him look older and wiser. His black framed glasses rested on a pointed nose that had the appearance of having been broken at least once. His hair was cut short and flowed seamlessly into his well-groomed beard. He wore a royal blue and black color-block polo shirt and a pair of black slacks, and a pair of sensible, no-skid black shoes. The whole ensemble might have seemed a bit nerdy, if it wasn't for his muscular frame and a pair of bright, gold-colored eyes. He reminded me of the actor, Chris Hemsworth.

"Hi Den, this is the new manager, Kat Normand," Babs said by way of introduction.

"Nice to meet you," he said, and held out his hand.

I took his hand but didn't follow through with the handshake. I was momentarily flustered by this man's handsome physique, and I felt a blush creep up my cheeks. He didn't quite fit the stereotypical *IT guy* model. He was strong and confident, and I found it hard to believe that he let Babs get away with picking on him.

Apparently, he didn't, though.

"Babs, call me Den again and I'll be sure to put a virus on your computer that will turn all of your icons into ducks that quack when you click on them," he said coolly, taking his hand back from me.

"Fine," she said, throwing her hands up in frustration.

"Now what was this about gibberish?" he asked again.

I explained to him about the minutes—how when I had read them at home last night, they hadn't made any sense, yet when I opened them again in the office to show Babs, the text was back to normal. Hearing myself say it all out loud, I began to wonder if I had imagined the gibberish in the first place.

"Hmm . . ." He seemed to be seriously mulling over my story. "Once I get you logged into your computer, we can look at the original digital file of the minutes and see if there is something going on with them." And with that, he gestured toward my own office.

"You believe me?" I asked as we walked into the office together.

"I believe that we can see what was in the original file."

"Okay, well I guess that's a starting point."

Ned took a seat at my desk, and I pulled one of the visitor chairs around so that I could look over his shoulder while he worked. Over the next half hour or so, he helped me to set up all of my applications, get logged into my computer, and configure my voice mail. He showed me how to connect to the printer and how to access my files from home or remotely. He then slid a drawer out on the left-hand side of the desk and pulled out a laptop.

"You are actually working off of a laptop, it's just docked into the monitor and keyboard. There is a carrying bag and travel charger over there in the cabinet." He pointed at my credenza.

"When you come back to the office, stick the laptop back into this drawer and it will charge and connect to the docking system wirelessly. It's got a two-terabyte solid state hard drive, so you shouldn't need to upgrade anytime soon."

"That's incredible! My cellphone can do something like that, but I've never heard of a laptop that could do it!" I exclaimed.

"This is proprietary technology; David Armstrong custom designed it for us. He used to be a computer engineer for NASA."

I gaped at Ned in disbelief. The patent for this type of technology could sell for more money than I would ever have in a lifetime, and yet this laptop was just sitting in my desk in an HOA in southern Virginia.

"Will he sell this technology? Is it available on the market somewhere?" I asked.

"No, he just designs this tech as a hobby. He's pretty much retired. He and I have had some great conversations over beers from time to time," Ned said, and shrugged.

"A hobby?" I repeated. "What kind of person does this sort of thing as a hobby and doesn't want to get paid for it?"

"A lot of the retirees around here have similar hobbies. I think that some of them have signed non-compete clauses with their companies or something," he explained.

Ned got all of my equipment set up in record time. He even configured an app on my cellphone so that I could make and receive calls from the HOA phone number rather than give out my personal cellphone number. When he finished setting everything up, he then began to click around in the Windows Explorer file browser on the computer.

"What are you looking for?" I asked.

"I wanted to double check the files of those minutes that you were reading," he said, and keyed the word *January* into the search field at the top of the screen. Sure enough, the search engine found the file folder that Odeon had named "Minutes." Ned then drilled down into the file until he found the file labeled *January 2023* and opened it.

I jumped up out of my seat and shouted, "There, see? It's nonsense!"

Ned scrolled up and down through the document and looked carefully at each page. It was riddled with red squiggly lines and blue double underlines on just about every other word; the spellcheck appeared to have highlighted more than half the document.

"I see it," he said, and continued scrolling through the pages as if doing so would suddenly make what he was looking at make sense.

"What's all the yelling about," Babs said as she barged into the office.

"Come look at this!" I exclaimed, and gestured her over to the computer. She leaned over Ned's shoulder, which was quite difficult for her given how short she was and how tall he was.

"Is it just this document? Are the other months the same way?" she asked.

Ned opened the files from the other five months, and everything appeared to be in the same gibberish. Then, for good measure, he also opened the October minutes; as expected, they were completely fine. I then asked him to check the June minutes, but there was no file for June on this computer since this machine hadn't been used since Odeon disappeared.

"Is it a computer virus?" Babs asked.

"Not possible. We have the best anti-virus software that money can't buy," Ned explained. "There's no way it's a virus." He navigated back to the explorer and right-clicked on the file to view its properties. "According to the metadata, it's the original file. And it hasn't been changed or modified since it was created in November of last year," he added.

I went over to the conference table and grabbed the binder of minutes from the tote, flipping through it until I found the minutes from the time period in question. Now when I looked at the pages, it was clear that there was nothing on them but a bunch of Lorem-Ipsum-type gibberish. I whipped the binder around and tilted it in the direction of the desk so that Babs and Ned could see the pages.

"See, I told you there was something wrong here. It's like someone tried to cover up the fact that these six months' worth of minutes are nothing but the rantings of a lunatic. Somehow, they managed to hide that fact. And now, for some reason, whatever they did is no longer working! Who could have done this and how?" I was nearly shouting.

"That's not good," Babs said. "If these are the *real minutes* then what did the board read and vote to approve? How could they possibly have mistaken that nonsense for the real deal?"

"That's a good question," Ned said. "But I think a more important question is, what the hell was going on with Arty back then? This isn't his style, he's usually so meticulous. Plus, I didn't think Arty would take the minutes. Don't we hire a scribe?" he asked Babs.

"We do hire a scribe, but Arty said she wasn't available for a little while and said that he would just take the minutes until she came back. Although . . ." Babs paused thoughtfully, "when Margery came back, I asked her how her trip was, and she had no idea what I was talking about. She said that Hilary Wen had asked her to take some time off but didn't explain why."

"Can the secretary do that—I mean without the support of the general manager or a vote of the full board?" I tried to recall the Bylaws.

"I guess," Babs answered. "We don't have a specific policy or governing document that refers to the use of a scribe. It's just something that we have been doing ever since Arty became the general manager. He argued that having a scribe would be a good way to keep the minutes professional and from being impacted by bias."

Babs explained that Margery was excellent at her job and that she also sometimes served as the parliamentarian for the board. Since the board was governed by volunteers, she helped everyone to stay on track with policy and procedure. Very early in his career, Arty had insisted on hiring someone, and he and Margery had worked well together.

"I wonder if any of this has something to do with Odeon's disappearance?" I asked out loud.

"Well, it does coincide with the months that Arty was acting erratically," Babs remarked.

"Did anything major happen to him around that time?" I asked.

"Didn't he get into that boating accident?" Ned asked Babs.

"Oh yeah," Babs said. "There had been that big October storm, right around Halloween. For some reason, he had taken the association's pontoon boat out onto the water that night. He never told me why. Anyway, he got stranded out in the rocky shallows in the middle of the lake. The storm had knocked out cell service and he wasn't able to call for help until morning," Babs explained.

She went on to say that the morning after the storm, Chief Baxter and Donny Roget had taken one of the police boats out onto the lake to rescue Arty. When they found him, his boat had taken on water and had nearly sunk. Inexplicably, Arty had been holding a soggy bundle of towels and muttering about rescuing a bird; he had refused to let go of it. Ultimately, they had loaded him and his bundle onto the police boat and then towed his busted rig back to the main marina. Arty had disappeared into his office before the chief could get an explanation from him about why he had been out on the water during a storm in the first place.

"If I recall correctly, he made a phone call right when he got back to his desk," Babs said. "It sounded almost like his ex-wife was on the phone. She has an exceptionally loud voice that always broadcast her side of the conversation, even if I wasn't trying to listen in."

I got the impression that Babs was always *trying* to listen in to other people's phone calls. I made a mental note to be sure to shut my door whenever I needed to make a private call.

"His ex-wife? But I thought that you said he was estranged from her?" I asked.

"He was," Babs said, and shrugged.

"I remember that boat wreck. The chief asked me to pull the security camera footage to see what might have happened, since he couldn't get a straight answer from Arty. The chief said that Arty was lucky to be alive; the pontoon boat was sinking, and they only barely managed to tow it back to the boat ramp."

"Well, that could explain Arty's change in behavior," I mused. "I mean, he could have experienced something traumatic and that could have triggered the erratic behavior." I crossed my arms and looked to Babs and Ned for confirmation of my theory. They both shrugged noncommittally. I wasn't expecting them to be experts in human behavior, but his strangeness and Arty's acting-out should have clued anyone in that there had been a problem.

"Maybe I should call Chief Baxter with this new information," I said.

"Well, you could," Babs said, "but you aren't going to tell him anything that he doesn't already know. All we've discovered was that Arty's boat accident occurred right before he apparently started going crazy."

"It's more than that, though," Ned said thoughtfully. "Someone made the effort to somehow conceal the fact that the minutes were nonsense. It's almost as if someone didn't want anyone to know *just how crazy* Arty was becoming until it was too late."

"But I still don't understand *how* they hid the wonky minutes," I said. "When I looked at the binder last night, I was certain that there was nothing but a bunch of random text there. Then I brought them back into the office this morning, and the text was back to normal." I threw my hands in the air in frustration. I was certain that if I could figure out the *how* then I might figure out the *why.* Perhaps it was some invisible ink that changed when exposed to different air temperatures or something.

Babs and Ned looked pointedly at each other, as if they knew something that I didn't.

"What?"

"It was an illusion," Ned explained. "One that was designed only to work while the binder was here in the office, but the second it was removed from here, the illusion disappeared."

"How does that even work? I've never heard of such a thing." I squinted at the two of them in annoyance. I wasn't in the mood for jokes or pranks. "And if that *is* the case, then why did the illusion disappear after we discovered the actual computer files? Once we saw the original digital file, it was as if the paper version of the minutes reverted to gibberish."

"There's a lot of stuff like that around here." Babs waved away my concerns. "We have a lot of people who used to be really talented in their former super-secret government jobs, and now they have the skills to make things seem strange and mysterious."

That didn't really explain anything to me, but I wasn't going to press the point at this moment. It was clear to me that there was something going on they weren't telling me. I would try and get to the bottom of it later.

"Okay . . . so it's an illusion, something someone did to try and hide that Arty was crazy. But why? What does anyone have to gain by hiding his mental health issues? Could it have been Arty himself?"

"No," Babs and Ned said simultaneously.

"No, Arty didn't have the skills to make such an illusion," Ned clarified.

"Well, who does?"

"There are several people in town," Babs explained. "But only a few of them might have a legitimate reason to want to do so." She tapped her finger on her chin in thought. "Arty's ex-wife is one of them. She had both the means and the motive, but did she have the opportunity?"

"Motive, opportunity? You sound like some cop show. We aren't *investigating* this; Chief Baxter and Detective Daniels are."

"No, you're right. *We* aren't investigating this," Babs teased, "but you are. You can deny it all you want, but I can read it on your face. You're not going to let this go until you figure out what happened to Arty."

"Can you blame me!" I protested. "I mean it's been four months, and the cops haven't discovered anything. I could be next! I mean, what if it has something to do with the job, with the general manager position? If you were in my shoes, wouldn't you want to figure this out, too?"

"Chill out," Babs said. "We're not judging you; we get it."

I took a deep breath and calmed myself down.

"This is exciting and all," Ned interrupted, "but I need to get going; I have to fix the security cameras at the back entrance to the Agora. Some critter chewed through the low voltage wires last night." And with that, he pulled my desk chair back, stood up, and walked out of the room, leaving just myself and Babs.

"So, tell me about the people that you believe have the means, motive, and opportunity." She was right: I wasn't going to let this go.

CHAPTER TEN

Babs and I talked about potential suspects for about an hour until reality caught up with us and she reminded me that we had a board meeting packet that was due in a few days.

I sat down at my computer and pulled up the agenda, intending to see what memos or documents I could get a jump on, but all I could think about was the short list of people that Babs thought could have had something to do with Arthur Odeon's disappearance.

At the top of the list there was his ex-wife, Robin Odeon. According to Babs, Robin was adept at the skills needed to create the illusion on the minutes. She was an artist of some sort and often incorporated illusions into her artwork. Babs described her work as mesmerizing.

Apparently, she mostly painted portraits of birds. The bird paintings were so lifelike, and Robin's illusions so realistic, that they gave the impression of flight. Robin had been especially upset after the divorce; Arthur had funded her obsessive collection of pet birds. She had fourteen: a conure, a pair of cockatoos, half-dozen parakeets, a macaw, a black and white pair of doves, and a pair of love birds. They were expensive to adopt and even more expensive to care for. Apparently, after the divorce, she had been forced to move into a small apartment above the garage of someone's home. It was the only place she had found that would permit her to keep her birds. Babs had overheard Robin telling Jessica that the apartment was way too small, and as a result it was loud and smelly. She missed the large house she had shared with Arthur, which had a large sunroom where she'd kept the birds' cages. Plenty of space, plenty of light, and separate enough from the main house that the birds didn't drive her and Arty insane. According to what Babs had overheard, she had exclaimed that she "would do anything to get that house back."

Next on the list was Jessica, the chief's fiancé. While she couldn't make illusion art like Robin could, she had the means and opportunity to have done something to Arty. Or she might have helped Robin with the plot to make her ex-husband disappear. I had to admit that I sensed a stone-cold attitude from Jessica, but it seemed like a stretch to say that she would abduct someone, or at worst, commit murder. She was, after all, engaged to the Chief of Police.

Babs then speculated that it could have been Clive. She believed that Clive had been mad at Arty for having shirked his responsibilities, and had even wanted to fire Arty, but the rest of the board hadn't backed him. But Babs had dismissed the idea of Clive being guilty almost immediately after she suggested it.

"After everything you told me, I would have fired Odeon if I had been in their shoes. Why didn't the board back Clive?" I asked her.

"I don't know, they had the conversation during a closed executive session and none of us were privy to the details. However, from what I understand, the counter-argument was spearheaded by Hilary Wen. She had somehow convinced enough of the board members to back off from the idea of firing him, and so Arty kept his job. Or so Arty told me."

I had asked Babs when this had taken place, and she explained that it was at the executive session just before the February board meeting. She said that from that point on, Clive had been acting very strangely—not just when he talked to Arty but in general. I then asked her if he was one of those madcap former scientists or engineers that could have made the illusion. It wasn't one of his skills that she knew of, but she mentioned that he was a collector of rare books, speculating that he may have known someone who could have pulled off the trick.

As I mulled over her theories, it all seemed based on conjecture. The closest plausible suspect was the ex-wife. Robin had more than enough reason to want Arty out of the picture, and she seemed to have at least some of the means to have conducted the coverup. But could she have pulled off the whole caper? She didn't really seem smart enough. I mean, I had never met the woman, but Babs was convinced that she was a dim bulb. On the other hand, Jessica was studying to become an attorney and, according to Babs, was a smart cookie; no one in their right mind would ever call her dumb—not if they wanted to live to tell about it. It was also plausible that the two of them together could have pulled off the crime.

Clive . . . well, he had been odd. The way he kept his car at a stifling 90 degrees and yet still dressed in layers, as if he had something to hide. But he seemed nice enough. It was clear that he adored his granddaughter, that alone gave him too much to lose. I couldn't imagine him even considering causing someone harm, let alone coming up with a wild plot to do away with a body.

I sighed and dragged my mind back to the present and the task at hand. The agenda was a short one, compared with the ones that I had been accustomed to back home. There was a motion to approve the purchase of a new lawn mower, a motion to approve the final version of a regulation change regarding the dress code for the fitness center, and a presentation from the garden club on the proposed fall landscaping design.

I already had everything I needed to complete the work. Willow had emailed me all the information I needed to draft up the memo and resolution for the purchase of the lawn mower. According to Babs, there were no major changes to the proposed regulation amendment from the board's previous discussion, so it was just a matter of refreshing the memo from the June meeting. She showed me where to find the templates for everything, and the two of us worked together to draft up all of the documents for the board packet.

Once the work was complete, she uploaded everything to a shared drive and sent an email to the board members letting them know that the documents were available. All the board members had their own laptops and could access PDF versions of the documents. It was a very modern and professional set-up; I was thrilled to see how it worked. It was often difficult to get people to part with their paper documents. Most HOAs certainly loved to kill trees for books and records; thankfully Blackwater Lake HOA seemed to be different.

The rest of the day passed uneventfully; I continued to review the governing documents in an effort to get caught up on the business of the association. I emailed Ned and asked him to give me access to Arty's old emails and correspondence. I had access to his files, but for some reason the emails hadn't been transferred over. Ned said he wouldn't be able to get to it until the next day, as he was still out in the field fixing the computerized inventory system for the Roanoke.

I sighed and decided that I would go old-school and read through some of the paper documents. I found a stack of newsletters that spanned from April of this year all the way back for about two years. When I asked Babs about the newsletters, she explained that there was a volunteer committee responsible for collecting the content, laying it out, editing it, and submitting it electronically to Babs so that she could send it to the printer. Arty had always reviewed the final proofs before they went to press, just to make sure they were good to go. With Arty gone, Babs hadn't felt comfortable giving the committee the stamp of approval, and Clive hadn't really been interested in doing it, so the newsletter had been suspended.

The newsletters were filled with community-based articles about fundraisers, events, clubs, and activities. The first few pages included information about the association business—meeting minutes and agendas, etc. As I flipped through the past issues, I realized quickly that there were no minutes published for the same six-month period during which Arty had been typing up nonsense. They reappeared in normal fashion when I went back as far as October.

"Babs?" I called.

"Yeah?" she said, poking her head into my office.

"Didn't anyone complain or say something about the minutes that were missing from the newsletter? I mean, it seems rather obvious—these issues are nearly four pages shorter than previous editions."

"They did ask about them, but Arty talked to them, and in most cases, people were content to come and read the minutes here in the office, the ones in the binder." She shrugged.

"That didn't seem strange to you?" I asked.

"You have to understand, it was all very strange then. Nothing Arty did seemed to be normal. He had been progressively taking a trip on the wacky train, but by March I had pretty much given up trying to figure him out. I just did my job and didn't ask questions."

"Well, promise me that if I start taking a trip on the 'wacky train' that you won't give up so easily. Please make as much of an effort as possible to figure out what is going on with me." I still feared that whatever had happened to Odeon could happen to me as well.

"Sure, sure. I wouldn't worry about it," Babs said, brushing my comments off. "You're not like Arty, you've got nothing to worry about. Why would anyone want to do something to you? After all, you only just got here."

I sighed and shoved the stack of newsletters back on the shelf in the cabinet. How on earth was I going to get anything done here? I was convinced that despite having spent the last two days reading all the documents that I could, I was way out of the loop on everything that was going on here. I couldn't explain it, and I had no evidence, but I just knew that there was more going on in this community than people were sharing.

First, there was the business of this *illusion*. While it was possible that there was some new and exciting technology out there that could scramble and rewrite the printed minutes, it was unlikely that such tech would be hidden away here in Virginia, rather than going mainstream in the tech market. Plus, I had worked in Northern Virginia all my adult life; being right outside of Washington, DC, it was the hub of government contractors. I knew plenty of scientists, engineers, and software developers, and none of them even remotely had the skills that Babs and Ned had described. They were just people, normal people. If they did work on top-secret projects, then it wasn't something that they were allowed to talk about or bring home to work on. *Illusion technology* seemed like one of those things that wouldn't be allowed to leave the laboratory or base. Never mind the fact that Ned and Babs couldn't seem to agree on whether it *was* technology, or if the illusion was some form of artistry. They had refrained from getting too specific about any of it.

Then there was the slow and gradual way that people were doling out information to me. It was almost painful to try and figure out what was going on around here. Babs had given me the minutes, and I had found and read the newsletters, but it really seemed as if everyone was waiting for me to ask about something before they divulged the relevant information. And when I did ask, it was almost a calculated and measured dose of information I was given, as if they were trying not to overwhelm me with all the details at once. However, if that was indeed the case, it was making my job more difficult. I had expected that there would be a learning curve and some disorientation—after all, it was only my second day at work—but this was beyond what I would call reasonable. I felt the rat's nest of anxiety tangling knots in my stomach again.

Maybe my colleagues were not the problem; maybe it was me. I had been accustomed to having the support of a management company behind me, and this was my first solo job. I felt I had to prove that I could handle this all by myself. It was lonely at the top. Maybe I wasn't cut out for it. Maybe I had been spoiled by having a network of professionals to lean on whenever I needed a sounding board or guidance on how to handle one situation or another. Now, I was stuck here trying to figure it all out on my own, like a hiker without a map. And this self-defeating train of thought wasn't going to do me any good. In fact, it was only likely to speed me on my journey to the "wacky train," just like Odeon.

Around lunch time, Babs popped into my office and asked me if I wanted to go up to the Shopette and get a sandwich from the cooler. I glanced down at my phone, and I realized that it was nearly one p.m. My stomach growled as if chiding me for forgetting to feed myself on time.

We locked up the offices and headed upstairs. The cooler in the Shopette had a selection of ready-made sandwiches and salads. I found a delicious looking tuna wrap that included avocado, fresh diced tomatoes, and sprouts. I *loved* sprouts in a tuna sandwich, and it was almost impossible to find places that included them. Celery and lettuce sure, but sprouts were almost unheard of in most restaurants. I grabbed the sandwich and a Greek yogurt with honey from the cooler and walked up to the counter to pay for my lunch.

"Do you just want me to add this to your tab?" Alice asked.

"You keep tabs here?" I responded.

"Yes, for both members and employees. For employees, we deduct the balance from each paycheck. Members get a monthly charge to their credit card on file."

"That could be dangerous," I said, making small talk.

"How so?" Alice asked, perplexed.

"There's so much good food and coffee here that I might just run up a tab that is higher than my paycheck," I quipped.

Alice giggled and keyed my items into the register.

"What is your pin number?" she asked. I turned to Babs, who had just walked up behind me. I still hadn't been given my pin number yet. This was yet another example of the painfully slow issuing of critical information.

"Just put it on mine," Babs said. Alice shrugged and keyed in a number that she had apparently memorized. Alice bagged up our lunch, and Babs and I took our lunches back down into the office suite. Both of us sat down to eat at the conference table in my office.

"I really do need a pin number," I told Babs. "How do I get one?"

"I need to issue one to you and then Ned activates it in the system. I'll send him an email today, and I'm sure he will take care of it tomorrow. He said he was busy in the field for the rest of the afternoon."

"Yeah, that's what he said when he replied to my email earlier today. Why does it seem like there is such a slow process for onboarding people around here? Is it always like this? I mean, a pin number seems like something you should have ready to issue to someone on their first day of work."

"It's a little complicated, but it's just the way people are around here. They want to be asked for something and won't generally volunteer information. They're very tight lipped." Babs took a bite of her blue-cheese apple vinaigrette salad.

"I noticed," I said, frowning. "I can't say that I like it. I feel as if I am being kept in the dark, like there's always some little piece of information that I'm missing. What's with all the secrecy?"

"You'll get used to it," Babs said. "Once people get to know you, they'll be a little more open with you, but you're still a stranger to everyone here. It's just going to take a while."

"Babs, you and I have been exchanging emails and phone calls for months now. It's not like we're strangers, but even you seem to keep things close to the vest!"

"Well, old habits die hard."

Babs changed the subject to work-related topics, mainly the events scheduled for this coming weekend. There was a concert scheduled to be held on the lake. The band would be on a barge floating out in the water and members could watch from the beach, clubhouse deck, or their boats.

"What's the name of the band?" I asked.

"Bare Naked Blowfish," she said, and I almost choked on my tuna wrap in response.

"Come again?" I asked.

"It's a cover band that plays music from the late last millennium. You know, Bare Naked Ladies, Hootie and the Blowfish, the Dave Mathews Band, Red Hot Chili Peppers, etc." she explained.

"The late last millennium?" I asked, feeling old.

"Yeah, the 1990s and early 2000s." She said this casually, as if she hadn't just lumped my teen and young adult years into some ambiguous-era classification. Babs was older than I was by a couple of decades, and I got the impression that she was messing with me. I chose not to react to her antics.

"Sounds like fun!" I said. "Was that what you meant when you warned Jet that he couldn't go to the concert?"

"Yeah, that scamp enjoys all the attention he gets from the crowds of people there. It's almost impossible to keep him away from the bigger events," she explained.

"What's the deal with him? Who owns him?" I asked. I really wanted to know. It seemed as if the pup had taken a liking to me, and if he was going to keep turning up at my house, then I wanted to know who he belonged to.

"Well, he grew up right outside of the community, but he always finds his way here in the HOA more often than not," she explained. "We all know him and look out for him. He never causes trouble, and we make sure he gets to where he needs to be."

"I should probably reach out to his owners and introduce myself so that I can bring him back home next time he pays me a visit."

"That's not necessary; you're better off just calling me or sending him on his way if you can't reach me. He knows his way around here and will find his own way home."

"Is his home so bad that he wants to escape it all the time? Do they neglect him or abuse him?"

"He's not abused, and neglect isn't the right word. He gets fed and everything, but it's really the community that takes care of him. It's complicated, but it's not something you need to worry about."

That was easier said than done. Here was this adorable dog, clearly an intelligent, loveable, and high-energy pup, who was roaming all over the neighborhood. No one seemed to be taking any responsibility for him. I just pictured him getting hit by a car or attacked by a wild animal. No dog deserved that; every dog deserved a happy and healthy home. I was getting frustrated by the cryptic way that Babs kept evading my questions. I made a mental note to try to ask the chief about Jet; he would have some additional information.

Babs and I finished our lunches and then went back to work. We wrapped up our day with some boring paperwork and administrative tasks that had been put off for a while, since the HOA hadn't had a general manager. The everyday busy work took up the better part of the afternoon.

Back at the house, I had half expected to find Jet on my porch again, and I wasn't disappointed. The springer spaniel was once again sitting in the Adirondack chair by the door, tail thumping as he beamed with excitement at my arrival.

"Hello again, you," I said as I unlocked the door.

I didn't even have to invite him in this time, he just hopped off the chair and followed me into the house. As we entered, he paused and peered into the small spare bedroom. He sniffed around for a minute and looked up at the ceiling as if he was taking note of the model planes and the mural.

"What is it boy?"

I asked. He whined a little and sat on his haunches, looking up at me.

"This room kind of creeps me out, too," I said. "I don't really know what it is about this room, but it makes me feel sad." I then turned out of the room and gestured for the dog to follow.

We walked down to the kitchen, and I grabbed a sparkling water from the refrigerator. I glanced longingly at the wine bottle on the counter but decided that I would wait until bed. I found that having a glass of red wine at night helped to relax me enough to fall asleep, and with all the stress lately, I could really use a little relaxation.

Taking my sparkling water and my cellphone, Jet and I walked out the back door and headed down to the dock at the edge of the lake. Penny should be home in about a half an hour, and my plan was to give her a call this evening and catch her up on everything that had happened. I would certainly get an earful from her because I hadn't called yesterday. It was a wonder that she hadn't sent out the National Guard yet.

As I approached the dock, I realized that there was someone sitting in one of the chairs overlooking the water. Jet must have seen them as well, because he began to growl under his breath and his fur stood upright on his back. How the heck did anyone get down there? As far as I knew, the only way into my backyard was through the house. The surrounding property was steep and overgrown with wildflowers and blackberries. There wasn't a direct path from the front to the backyard. I froze in my tracks, trying to assess the situation. Whoever they were, Jet didn't seem to like them very much.

"Hello?" I called out. The person in the chair looked up from what they were holding, which I could see now was a tablet or phone. They stood up and turned around to face me. The person was backlit by the setting sun and their face was in shadow, but I was fairly certain that I knew who it was.

"Hilary?"

"Hello there," she said, and she smiled and waved at me. I moved a little bit closer so that I could see her face more clearly.

"Can I help you with something?" I now knew that it was one of the board members, but I was still wary.

"Well, no. I just thought I would stop by and see how you were adjusting. I know it's your second day, and all. The board packet that you sent out today looked very good. You certainly seem to have hit the ground running."

"Um . . . yeah, it was no big deal, really. Babs was a big help. I couldn't have done it without her."

"Yes, I heard that you are looking into the disappearance of Arty Odeon." It wasn't really a question.

"No, I mean not really. I'm just curious, I guess; worried that whatever happened to him might happen to me." Having come from a large county, I wasn't comfortable with the way that gossip traveled so quickly in this community. I hadn't even realized that was what I was doing until this morning, when Babs and Ned had accused me of investigating.

"Well, I just wanted to let you know that it's not necessary. The chief and Detective Daniels are on the case, and you don't need to snoop around."

"I'm not snooping!"

Jet yipped as if in affirmation.

"You are, and there's no need. Stay in your lane. Don't worry about any of this." Hilary's expression was momentarily dark and stern, but she suddenly beamed a big friendly smile at me. It was as if someone had flipped a switch.

"Really though, it's just that you have so much to take in and learn here, and it's only your first week. I don't want you to be over-whelmed," she cooed as if I was an upset child.

"Thanks," I said flatly. I didn't buy it. If anyone was snooping it was her. She seemed to be here to try and gather more information about what I've been up to. It all seemed like another layer of secrecy around this strange community.

"In any case, there's no need for you to worry. From what I've heard, I'm certain that you're not in any danger, at least not like Arty was." She paused thoughtfully. "Unless you keep snooping, and then who knows what will happen?"

Was that a threat? Jet seemed to think it was, because he growled low under his breath.

"Anyhoo!" she exclaimed, flipping that switch again and chan-neling her cheery persona. "I need to get going. Toodles!" She waved at me as she walked up the path toward my house.

I watched her for a minute, trying to determine how she'd got into the yard, and how she would get out of it. She veered to the right of the house, rounded the corner, and then disappeared. I let out a breath that I hadn't realized I had been holding. Jet whimpered a little at my side and looked up at me almost apologetically.

"Some guard dog you are—you couldn't have given me a heads up that she was back here?" I scolded. "Was that suspicious or what?"

We walked down to the dock and each of us took an Adirondack chair. I scrolled through my phone, catching up on emails and social media, biding my time until I could call Penny.

CHAPTER ELEVEN

"Wait, wait. Rewind. You're talking way too fast," Penny said, interrupting my rant as I tried to catch her up on everything that had happened. The moment she'd answered my video call, I dove straight into my story, not giving her a chance to scold me for not calling her yesterday. I took a deep breath and started again, slowly explaining everything that had happened over the past two days.

"Your IT guy is hot?" she asked.

"What! That's what you took from that *whole* story—that Ned is hot?" I sputtered.

"Well, yeah, but you don't seem as interested in him as you are in the chief. Is Ned already taken?"

"No—I mean I don't know, I didn't ask him. He is my *employee!*" I protested.

"Yeah, but the chief is taken, so he's off limits. Now you've got to keep fishing."

"I wasn't fishing in the first place. Stop trying to play matchmaker and pay attention! Something weird is going on here. Not just the disappearance of the old GM but all of it. I can't figure it out."

"Okay, let's start from the top. You discovered that the former GM had been slowly going mad for about six months before he disappeared, and that someone was covering it up. The cover-up was a high-tech illusion of some sort that only works in the clubhouse or office building . . . that technology is unusual, it almost sounds like magic. . . . And lastly, you discovered that Arty had written himself some sort of note saying to 'follow the bird' to South Beach," she summarized.

"Yeah, that's it, I guess. You just left off the part where the weird board member showed up at my house and made veiled threats … oh, and Jet."

"Jet?" she asked. "I don't remember anything about a jet."

"Not a jet, just Jet. He's an adorable English springer spaniel who seems to have adopted me, for some reason. He just keeps showing up at my house. I thought I told you about him already," I explained.

"You may have, but it didn't stick," she said, and I could almost hear her shrug.

"Right. Anyway, Jet was here tonight when Hilary, the board member, showed up, and he growled at her. Something's not right with that woman."

"Are you adding her to your list of suspects?" Penny asked.

"I'm not keeping a list of suspects!" I protested.

"But you said that you and Babs had a short list of people. It sounds like you should add this Hilary woman to the list," Penny commented.

"I don't know. What would her motive be? I mean, sure she has the opportunity since she is a board member, but what about the means? Could she have pulled off the illusion thing? I really don't know anything about her," I sputtered, unsure why I was playing along with this notion of an investigation.

"But she already did pull off something like it. You said she seemed to disappear around the corner of your house, just like magic. You also said that there was no way she could have gotten up the hill to the driveway from that side of the house. Seems to me like someone who could make an illusion of some sort," Penny said.

"I don't know. I don't like Hilary, but that doesn't make her a bad guy. What do you think, Jet?" I said, and turned my phone so the camera could see the spaniel lazing about on the chair. "Do you think Hilary Wen could have something to do with Odeon's disappearance?"

Jet perked his ears, sat up straight, and yipped in the affirmative. I turned the camera back to myself.

"One: that dog is adorable, and Two: he completely agrees with me. You need to add Hilary to your suspect list."

I wanted to protest again that I didn't have a suspect list, but I knew it would fall on deaf ears.

Penny and I switched topics, and she caught me up on how the new tenant was doing in my townhome and how things were going on her end. At some point, Jet hopped off the chair, walked over, and sprawled across my feet. It was nice, especially since it started to get chilly once the sun set and the mosquitoes had come out. I wrapped up my phone call just as it got too dark for Penny to see me on the video, and Jet and I walked up to the house. I let us both inside.

"So, what's your plan, kiddo? Should I let you back out so that you can go home?" I asked him, unsure why I was bothering to ask the dog anything. Jet tilted his head in his endearing way and then hopped onto my couch, making himself comfortable.

"I guess you're staying in for the night," I said, scratching him behind the ears. Perhaps if he was missing overnight, his owners would reach out to try and find him. Surely, they would call the office at some point in time. He closed his eyes and fell asleep on the couch.

It was only eight-thirty, but I was exhausted from all that had happened over the past few days. I climbed the stairs to my loft bedroom, changed into pajamas, climbed into bed, and played on my phone for a while until I finally fell asleep.

In the morning, I woke up before my alarm went off. Jet was sitting at the foot of the bed, barking softly.

"Mfph . . . get off the bed, buddy." I nudged him off the bed with my foot. "I guess you need to go outside and pee." I hopped out of bed, went downstairs, and opened the front door to let him out. Jet darted off toward the clubhouse. For a moment, I felt a pang of guilt for once again not taking the time to find out who he belonged to, and for not putting him on a leash, but if Babs wasn't worried about him roaming around town, then I guessed everything would be okay.

I took a deep breath and enjoyed the cool morning air. The day would be another hot one, but at least the nights and mornings had started to cool down. I spun on my heels and turned back into my house, heeding my own call of nature before stumbling into the kitchen to make some coffee.

I showered and dressed and headed off on my walk to the office. This morning, I had the good sense to dig my messenger bag out of my bedroom closet where I had stashed it. It was one of the last items I had brought in from my car; it had carried my laptop and other gadgetry that I wanted to have handy upon arrival. Now, it held my laptop, my notebook, and the planner that Babs had foisted upon me. I had tried to convince her that digital was the way to go and that I would just access the calendar via my phone, but she wasn't hearing any of it. She promised to take my planner from me at the end of each day and ensure it was up to date. There really wasn't any way to convince her otherwise, so to keep the peace, I reluctantly agreed.

I was a little early, so I decided to go up to the restaurant's self-serve kiosk to get a second coffee for the day. Earlier this morning, Babs had texted me my new PIN number. I was so grateful not to be dependent on Babs. Looking around the restaurant, I felt as giddy and as intimidated as I had as a college freshman using the dining hall for the first time. Ultimately, though, it was as anticlimactic as you would expect. With my coffee and pastry in hand, I walked out of the restaurant and almost straight into Jessica.

"Watch where you are going!" she exclaimed, and looked down her nose at me. Her stiletto heels gave her enough added height that she seemed to tower over me, though she was probably around my height without them.

"I'm sorry, I was entranced by this delicious coffee. It's the best pumpkin spice brew I have ever had, and it doesn't even use those sickly sweet syrups," I said, trying to make small talk.

"What did you expect, some burnt sugar concoction like the big chain stores make? Brewmstick Roasters are the best in Virginia," she said haughtily.

"I guess I just hadn't had the chance to sample their fall flavors before I left Centreville. I'll have to make a note to add this to my grocery order," I said, ignoring her arrogance and trying to maintain a friendly disposition. After all, it was only my third day here, and I didn't need to make any enemies this early in the game.

"You do that," she said flatly before striding into the restaurant, clearly disinterested in further conversation.

"Jessica," I called after her, remembering that I had something that I wanted to ask her. She spun on her heels and turned back to me; arms crossed in impatience.

"What?"

"I heard that you are friends with Robin, Odeon's ex-wife. I just wanted to check and see if anyone from the association had reached out to her during these trying times. It must be really difficult for her." I was layering on as much sincere sympathy as I could.

"Why would it be difficult for her?" Jessica asked.

"Well, I understand that her breakup with Arthur was rather recent—within the past year or so—and I have heard through the grapevine that she wanted to reconcile."

"*She* wanted to reconcile things with *Arthur*?" Jessica said. "Not on your life. She was glad to be done with him. I doubt anyone from the association has reached out to her, and frankly, I doubt that she would even care if they did."

"Oh! I'm sorry if I offended, I should have realized that there are two sides to every story; but I had heard that she wanted to try and patch things up with him so that she could move back in with him. You know, because they co-owned the house?"

"It was his house. She didn't want it; she just wanted more space for her precious flock," Jessica explained.

"Is she going to inherit it? You know, once all the legal paperwork settles and he is presumed dead?"

"Unlikely, but I don't know what will happen to the house. My law firm isn't managing the will, but I'm sure he didn't leave it to Robin. Besides, she doesn't need it anymore; she's engaged and will move in with her new fiancé soon."

"Fiancé?" I was stunned. It was only my third day in town, but Babs seemed to have the tea on everyone in the area. It seemed unlikely that she would have overlooked this juicy bit of information.

"Yes, Ingus Pyrus. He's a senior engineer for one of the big science firms—you know, the ones that are sending celebrities into space? He's got a mansion on the same end of the lake where Odeon's house was located," she said matter-of-factly. It was clear that she was proud of the fact that she was able to one-up me with some new gossip.

"Oh, well. I was just worried that with the lack of leadership in the association, no one had even thought to check on her. I'm glad to hear that she is doing well," I said sincerely.

"Well, like I said, she couldn't care less about what the association has to say. I have a nine a.m. meeting with a client in the lounge. Excuse me." And with that, she spun around dangerously on her heels and strode away.

If I wore heels like that and tried that pirouette, I would have fallen flat on my posterior.

"Bye!" I shouted in the direction of her high-end-fashion-covered backside. I resumed sipping my coffee and made my way downstairs to the offices.

As I greeted Babs, I resisted the urge to tell her everything I had just learned, slightly torn between my excitement to share the news of the past twelve hours and confusion over what Babs was wearing. Finally, I gave in to my curiosity and asked her outright.

"Babs, what on earth are you wearing?"

She looked down at her clothes and then up at me, perplexed. She was dressed like the woman from the *American Gothic* painting by Grant Wood. She wore a burgundy dress printed with a pattern of tiny gold step-and-repeat diamonds, with a lace collar and a cameo brooch on the throat. Her short hair was parted in the middle and combed down to give the appearance of being pulled back severely. All she needed was a pitchfork and the image would be complete.

"What, this old thing? I bought this outfit at a craft fair in Richmond a few years back. I think the vendor was Amish or Quaker or something." She said this as if those groups were the same thing.

"You look like you're trying to be a caricature of Americana," I blurted out. Then, realizing what I'd said might be rude, I backpedaled: "Not that there is anything wrong with that."

"Thanks! That's the look I was going for," Babs said proudly.

I honestly couldn't tell if she was messing with me or if she was sincere, so I decided to move on.

"I ran into Jessica upstairs, almost literally, and she all but cleared Robin of any motive," I announced.

"Explain," Babs said bluntly, and gestured for me to continue. I spent the next half hour rehashing everything that had happened since I left work yesterday. My conversation with Jessica, the mysterious visit to my house by Hilary Wen, and Jet's sleepover on my couch.

"Well, that's disappointing," Babs said when I had finished telling her my tale. She plopped back down at her desk and turned to her computer.

"That's it, that's all you have to say?" I asked.

"Well, yeah, I mean, I had been certain that Robin was somehow part of Arty's disappearance, but clearly, she's not. The reference to the bird at South Beach seemed to be a dead giveaway, but obviously, she has no motive," she said.

"And that's the end of it? You are going to let it go?" I asked.

She paused in her typing and looked up at me, confused.

"Let what go? I thought you said that you weren't investigating this."

"I'm not!" I protested, a little too defensively, "but with Robin eliminated, that only leaves us with two potential people, and aside from being a little bit creepy, neither seems to have a motive."

"Us? You're the one who is investigating," Babs protested.

"Okay, fine, but what can you tell me about Clive or Hilary's relationship with Odeon? Did he get along well with them?"

"I don't know why you suspect Clive. There's no way on earth that man would hurt anyone; he's one of the sweetest guys I know. He's like a grandfather to everyone, genuinely nice."

"Well, it's just that I got some pretty weird vibes from him. Something's not quite . . ." I paused, "*right* with him. I just can't put my finger on it."

"It's certainly not abduction and murder."

"But—" I spluttered.

"It's not him," Babs said firmly.

"Okay, if it's not him, then let's talk about Hilary Wen. Why was she at my house? She was clearly there to make a threat. Even Jet growled at her, and he seems to be a fairly good judge of character."

"Jet is only a pup; I wouldn't put any stock in his actions," Babs said, but she was clearly thinking about my question. "I don't know why Hilary was at your house. You're right, it doesn't make any sense. She had no business being there. I don't even think she has a key. Clive and I had the only copies, and now you have Clive's set."

"And what about your set, do you still have them?" I asked, unsurprised by this; the association owned the house, after all.

"I do."

"Can you check on them? Where do you keep them? Maybe Wen borrowed them."

Babs stood up and walked over to the copy room, reaching behind the door to a key cabinet mounted on the wall. She pulled out a set of keys that were identical to mine, complete with the leather keychain and everything.

"They're still here. Doesn't look like they've moved," Babs said.

"This doesn't make any sense. How did she get into my backyard last night, and why? Was she just trying to keep me focused on my new job, or was she trying to distract me from the investigation?" I asked.

Babs crossed her arms and stared at me sternly, looking even more like a facsimile of the painting.

"What?"

"I thought you weren't investigating," Babs said.

"I'm not. I have work to do, and so do you," I said, and finally turned away from her desk to head into my office. I could hear her sit back down and clack away at her keyboard.

I strode into my office and tossed my messenger bag on the credenza behind my desk. I cued up my computer and opened my email account. My goal was to pick up where I had left off with the catch-up research I had started yesterday. I wanted to continue reading through Odeon's emails and files to get up to speed on the recent work of the association. I specifically wanted to know where we were with the budget and if any capital projects were underway.

As I worked, it occurred to me that I needed to meet with Willow to discuss her operational needs for the maintenance department and for any projects she was responsible for. I sent her a quick email requesting a meeting and made sure to copy Babs as well, since she had declared herself the keeper of my calendar. I wasn't used to having an admin assistant. I had always just done things for myself, or more often than not, I was the one who was responsible for keeping track of someone else's schedule. It would take a little getting used to, now that I was dealing with the reverse role.

I tried to focus on the task at hand, but my mind kept wandering back to Arthur Odeon's disappearance. I was increasingly worried that the same thing that happened to him would happen to me. It was really creepy the way Hilary Wen had made her way into my backyard. *The association owns the house, but that doesn't give her the right to just show up unannounced, does it?* I asked myself.

I pulled up Odeon's email archive, Ned had finally made it available, and I searched for Hilary Wen's name and email address. It wasn't long before I found what I was looking for: an email thread between Arthur and Hilary, dating to approximately six months before Odeon's disappearance. It was apparent in the emails that he was accusing her of something, but he hadn't seemed to want to elaborate on whatever it was in writing. Nevertheless, she appeared to know precisely what he was referring to and was unhappy about it. I read the email thread out loud to myself.

Hilary,

I know what you have been up to lately, how you have been making a little extra money. I saw your post on Claire's List. I've set up several internet alerts for the association since it's my job to protect and curate the brand image of this place. Lo and behold, one of those alerts led me to a link on Claire's List. Although it was anonymous, I know it was you. It had to have been you; the ad was filled with the same typos you make all the time. Did you think that no one would notice an ad on Claire's List?

~Odeon

Arty,

I can assure you that whatever add you came across has nothing to do with me. Im not sure what your angle for. What is it you want?
-H

Hilary,
I know that it was your ad, the typos in your last message just proved it to me. I saw some of the message traffic back and forth with the potential buyers. How long did you think you could keep up the ruse? You know the rules for living here; there are just some things you can't share on the internet. I will have to bring this to Clive's and Chief Baxter's attention. I have no angle other than that. I just wanted to give you the opportunity to fess up first; maybe they will go easy on you.
-Odeon

Arty,
Im done with this conversation. You do whatever you feel you have to do. I have nothing to hide.
-H

I printed the email thread and stared at the sheets of paper on my desk. What did it all mean? Was Hilary stealing something from the HOA and selling it on Claire's List? What were these "rules" that Clive was referring to? I didn't recall seeing anything in the governing documents that regulated internet or social media use. Frankly, it would be hard to regulate such things, especially given the First Amendment rights of this country.

I tried another keyword search, this time for Claire's List, and found automatic messages from the site notifying Odeon of a status update for an ad he was following. The notifications showed snippets of message traffic between him and the seller. It looked as if Arthur Odeon had created an alias on the website to try and engage with the seller; the handle was in a different name. I clicked on the links in the emails, hoping to view the ad and the entire message traffic, but I was blocked by an error message page that informed me the ad was no longer available. I returned to my email search and tried to piece together the fragments of conversations.

As expected, there were the usual questions about how much something costs, the authenticity, and the sale logistics. I scrolled through the emails, most of which were in the deleted items folder and all of which were riddled with broken links. Very little, beyond the mundane, made sense. There was a reference to "proof" and another reference to "paranormal." The last email I clicked showed almost a complete sentence before the "click here to read more" link cut into it. It was a message from Hilary Wen to Arty Odeon.

"'He's a dragon, what else do you—'" I read aloud.

"Who's a dragon?"

I looked up and realized that Babs had come into the office.

"I don't know, I feel like I'm falling down the white rabbit's hole. None of this makes any sense!" I leaned back in my chair and swept my hands through my hair, pressing the palms of my hands into my eyes to try and stem the headache that was blooming.

"What are you working on?" Babs asked, coming around behind my desk. She leaned over my shoulder to read the email. "What am I looking at here?"

A moment later, she stepped back from my desk and leaned against my credenza, drumming her fingers on the surface. Her concerned expression and unusual outfit gave her the air of a stern school matron. With the word "dragon" tripping through my head, I felt like I was at Hogwarts School of Witchcraft and Wizardry and that Babs was Professor McGonagall, sans the pointy hat.

"It's email traffic between Hilary Wen and Arty Odeon. It appears that she was trying to sell something on Claire's List that belonged to the association. Perhaps many somethings," I explained.

"Okay . . . so what does a dragon have to do with it?" Babs asked hesitantly.

"I honestly don't know; it was in one of the messages and it fits with all the other strange fragments of sentences in these emails. Would the association happen to have had some sort of dragon statue, maybe a mascot or a relic?" I asked her.

She seemed to visibly relax in front of me, and her expression of consternation smoothed out into her ordinarily cheerful face.

"No, nothing like that. I'm sure I don't know what that sentence means by 'he's a dragon,'" she said cryptically.

"You're sure that you don't know?" I asked, raising an eyebrow.

"That's what I said," Babs answered. "Anyway, it doesn't look like you are getting much work done; I thought you were going to start drafting the Invitation for Bid to repair the park bathrooms? I just came in here to add something to your schedule." She reached for my planner.

"What are you adding?" I asked.

"The Ladies Auxiliary of Blackwater Lake has invited you to their luncheon tomorrow, upstairs in the Roanoke. You should attend. I can't protect your schedule for much longer, and this is at least a good group to start the introductions with."

"Protect my schedule?"

"Well, yeah. All the clubs and groups have been clamoring to invite you to their meetings and events. If they had their way, you would be booked every minute of every day, but Clive asked me to let you get settled in before the onslaught," she said, shrugging.

"Good grief," I groaned, pressing my palms to my eyes again. "Just how many people will be at this luncheon tomorrow?" I asked.

"Oh, a hundred, give or take."

"And you consider this to be the best choice for first introductions! You couldn't have started off with the ladies knitting club, or something?" I joked.

"Ha! No way. You wouldn't want to meet them first; they just might stab you with their knitting needles; you'd be lucky if you walked away without puncture wounds. You don't mess with the Knight Knitters."

"The Night Knitters?" I asked. "Do they only knit at night?"

"Knight, with a 'k;' they claim that some of their members have ancestors who knitted cloaks for the knights of the Crusade. Not that they can prove it," Babs explained.

"There's that word again, *proof*," I muttered.

"What was that?" Babs asked.

"Nothing, just thinking out loud," I said. "Thanks for the calendar update and for protecting my schedule as much as you have. What's the dress code for tomorrow?" I nearly slapped myself in the forehead when I realized who I was talking to.

"I actually don't know," Babs answered, to my relief. "You can give Jessica a call; she is the president."

I felt like slapping myself again.

"Great, yeah, I'll be sure to do that," I said.

"Do you need her phone number?" Babs asked, oblivious to my discomfort.

"No, I'm sure it's around here somewhere." I gestured at the desk and computer.

"Great. Let me know if you need help with that Invitation for Bid," Babs said, and hustled back out of my office. I could have sworn that she sighed in relief as she walked out the door. What did she have to be relieved about? It wasn't like she was the one who had to go to a luncheon with a hundred strangers led by the one and only Ice Queen herself, Jessica Cheverie. I was still unsure why she was treating me with such disdain, but I wasn't about to ask her about the dress code for this luncheon.

I turned back to my computer and stared at the strange sentence again. *He's a dragon.* What could it possibly mean? What was Hilary selling? And was she involved in Arty's disappearance?

CHAPTER TWELVE

I was distracted throughout the day; I would get a paragraph written on the Bid document, and then I would find myself running another keyword search through Odeon's emails and files. I would scold myself, get back to work, and stay focused for just long enough to complete a page. Eventually, I decided to distract myself from my own distractibility and picked up the phone. I looked up Willow in the community directory and dialed her phone number. She answered on the second ring.

"Hi Kat!" she said upon answering.

"Hey, Willow, would you have time to stop by my office and discuss the IFB for the park bathroom renovations? Some of the specifications you listed don't make any sense to me."

"Sure," she said, "I'll swing by in about fifteen minutes; I'm just up the road."

"Thanks." I hung up the phone. I needed to get up and walk around a bit, get away from my desk. I went to the Shopette and grabbed a bottle of water and some aspirin for my headache, then paid with my pin code.

"Say, Alice, would you happen to know what the dress code is for tomorrow's luncheon?" I asked.

"The Ladies Auxiliary luncheon? Sure! Are you going? If so, you'll have to sit at my table. I'll introduce you to everyone!"

"You will? That's awesome! What should I wear?" I prompted again.

"The August luncheon is always the White Luncheon. Just wear something white. After all, it will be your last opportunity to do so. No more white outfits after Labor Day, or so they say."

"White? All white, or can I just wear a blouse?" I asked.

"White pants are best; you can pair them with anything. I personally will be wearing white slacks with a white sleeveless blouse and a vintage 1990s red Chanel blazer with white piping. It was my mother's," she said, blushing.

The '90s are vintage? I was incredulous.

"Okay . . . thanks," I said, feeling another knot forming in my stomach. Did I actually own enough white clothing to put together an outfit? I walked out of the Shopette, opened the package of aspirin, and washed two of them down with water. As I stood in the foyer, Willow glided through the front door. Her tall, thin frame was backlit by the light shining through the windows.

"Hey, Kat!" she said cheerfully. "You didn't have to meet me up here; I was just on my way down to your office."

"Oh, no, I just stopped by the Shopette," I said, gesturing toward the store with the water bottle.

"Of course," Willow said.

"Shall we?" I led the way back downstairs.

At my office, Babs waved at Willow but didn't tease or heckle her as she had done previously. Willow and I sat down at the conference table and reviewed the specifications she had sent me about the bathroom renovations.

The rest of the afternoon passed quickly. I learned more about the special bathroom accommodations for our members than I would ever have wanted to know. Why we needed to invest in heated toilet seats that can be turned on with a foot pedal, or extra-large, self-cleaning cat litter boxes was beyond me. Still, the board had approved the budget for the project, and as a new hire I didn't feel like I was in a position to argue.

Willow and I wrapped up drafting the IFB, and she was just about to head back into the field when I decided to confide in her.

"Willow, do you know anything about a dragon?" I asked her, realizing that I probably sounded stupid. She stopped dead in her tracks, stepped back into my office, and shut the door behind her.

"What do you know about a dragon?" she said.

That was certainly not the answer I had expected.

"Not much, honestly—actually, nothing. I just saw a reference to it in one of Odeon's emails. I think someone may have stolen it and tried to sell it," I said, not wanting to reveal my suspicions about who had stolen it.

"Him, not it, and I can assure you that he hasn't been stolen," Willow said.

"So, you do know what the dragon reference means! Is it a mascot, or statue?" I asked, trying to think of why someone would call a dragon *him* instead of an *it*.

"No," Willow said flatly, without further explanation. She forced herself to relax, flashed a bright smile, and said, "There's no need to worry. Whatever email you found must not have meant what you thought. Nothing has been stolen that I'm aware of, and I would know. I keep the inventory of all the association's belongings." She reached out and patted my shoulder. "See you later." And with that, she spun around and wisped right out of the room. I barely noticed her opening the door and closing it behind her again.

I was speechless. What on the good green Earth was going on here? It was becoming evident that the reference to a dragon had some credibility, but no one could (or would) tell me what it meant. The only thing that was clear to me was that the dragon was likely a person and not a thing. If Hilary Wen hadn't stolen something, what *had* she been trying to sell on the internet? What could be so intangible and yet require proof and authentication? I needed more information; the answers to these questions were right at my fingertips, but I just couldn't grasp them.

I wasted more of my afternoon searching for more evidence on the computer, but my keyword searches no longer yielded usable results. I kept bumping into the same four or five emails. I needed to broaden my search terms, but my brain was fried from exhaustion and frustration. Instead, I decided to create an account with an alias on Claire's List and see if I could message Hilary Wen's seller profile. According to her profile, she hadn't actively posted anything for sale in about eight months but hadn't closed the account. I felt as if she was biding her time and waiting for the law enforcement scrutiny to let up so she could return to selling whatever she had stolen.

I drummed my fingers on the desk as I contemplated what to write, then clicked the button that read "Message this Seller" and began typing:

Username: BauerBronco91
  Subject: Still Available?
  Message: Dear seller, I came across an old screenshot that someone sent me of one of your expired Claire's List posts. It intrigued me and I wanted to see if it was still available. Can you please tell me more about the dragon? Has it been sold?

I hovered my mouse over the send button. Was there anything in this message that could give me away? My screen name and email address were ones that I had used ages ago, back when Yahoo Messenger and AOL Instant Messenger were still popular. I never used them in my everyday correspondence now. They weren't on my resumé or my social media accounts, so it was unlikely that she could connect them with me. Still, I hesitated. If Hilary was behind Odeon's disappearance, she could be a threat. I felt my stomach tighten and fear return to me; it was that feeling that had been with me since Saturday when I had first learned about the disappearance of the former GM. It was the fear that I was in danger, that I was next.

"Well, if I don't take any action to find out who is behind this, and try to stop them, I could be the next one to disappear," I rationalized with my flawed logic.

Hands shaking, I hit the send button.

I stood up to stretch and paced around my office, trying to shake off my apprehension. As I reached down for my bottle of water, I heard the door to my office open behind me. I jumped and spun around, startled.

"Sorry, didn't mean to scare ya," Babs said. She walked purposefully over to my desk, paying me no mind, and picked up my planner.

"Just came in to make one last check in your planner before I head out," she explained.

"Is it five o'clock already?"

"Yep, I'm headed home, and you should too. You've got no reason to stick around here after five. Besides, you're going to need to rest up."

"Why do I need to rest up?" I asked, confused.

"Because you'll need to muster all your energy to deal with the flock of hens tomorrow at the luncheon. They are going to swarm you with questions and project proposals."

"I thought you said this was the easy group for introductions?" I asked.

"It is."

"Oh, Lord. That bad, huh?" I asked.

"Why do you think I've never joined them? Besides the fact that I don't look good in white."

I scowled at her. Babs had told me earlier that she didn't know the dress code for the event. Well, if that was the game she was playing, then at least I was onto her now. I remembered my first day here and the book she had been reading, *The Art of Managing Up*; everything was starting to click.

"Well then, I guess it's a good thing that I spoke with Alice earlier. She told me the dress code and promised to introduce me to all the important people." I winked at her.

"She did?" Babs said, seeming both impressed and disappointed.

"Yep, promised that I could sit at her table and everything. I'm sure she will help keep the hen pecking to a minimum," I said, coolly.

"Well, okay then," Babs said, her tone slightly defeated. She put my planner back on my desk and headed for the door. "I'll see you tomorrow." She chuckled as she walked out of my office. I thought she must be amused that she had a worthy opponent for her antics and games.

No longer shaking with my earlier nerves, I sat down at my desk, exhausted. I put my head down and closed my eyes. My headache was coming back. I should really head home, but I couldn't bring myself to move. Suddenly, I felt my cellphone buzz under my right elbow. It was a notification of an email message. I opened my Yahoo app and checked out the email. It was a reply to my message on Claire's List. Just three words:

Who is this?

The message was certainly not the response I had been expecting. At most, I thought Hilary would message me back and tell me the dragon was no longer available. Why did she respond this way? Had I somehow given myself away? Either the listing hadn't mentioned a dragon, or it hadn't been listed long enough to garner attention. She knew something was up. Did she suspect that it was me? I looked around the office in paranoia. How could she know, or even suspect? It was impossible; I was being absurd.

I stood up again, stretched, and packed my messenger bag to head home for the evening. I was done for the day. Done with work, done with playing amateur detective, and done with constant worry. All I wanted to do was to go home, have a glass of wine, and take a hot bath. I locked up the office and headed back up to the foyer.

I bumped into the chief and Jessica on my way out of the building. They were arm in arm and clearly headed to dinner in the Roanoke. They made such a lovely couple. He was tall, built, and handsome. His warm brown eyes and crew-cut hair made for a striking contrast to her ice-blue eyes and white-blond mane. I felt a pang of jealousy; he was way too good for her. I tried to stifle those thoughts; I was being absurd. I didn't even know him!

"Hey there!" Jay said cheerfully. "How have you been settling in?"

"Oh, hi," I sputtered in response. Jessica sneered at me and clutched Jay's arm tighter. "I'm settling in well. It's only my third day, but I feel like I know everyone already."

"Well, you won't feel that way tomorrow," Jessica said. "I hear you are attending the LAX luncheon." It was a statement, not a question. I really didn't get why she was so bitter toward me, but perhaps that was just her disposition.

"Why yes, I am." I smiled confidently. "I already have a table and everything; I'll be seated with Alice," I said.

"Alice French?" Jessica asked.

"Yes. I hear that she's well-connected. She's offered to introduce me to everyone."

"Well connected? If you consider that all of her connections were once her mother's. She's a legacy LAX member, second generation. It's the only reason she was elected vice president and serves as an officer."

"Jessica. Be nice. Alice is knowledgeable and well organized, from what I hear," Jay said.

"Oh, I don't doubt it. Alice seems like the type of person who gets things done and treats people kindly," I said, glaring at Jessica. She glared back, and we stared icily at each other for a few moments.

"Well, it was good to catch up with you, Kat, but Jessica and I have dinner reservations," Jay said, gently tugging his fiancé's arm.

I turned and watched them walk away and then headed home. I walked up the trail, checking my phone to see if I had any more emails from Claire's List. I hadn't responded to the first one, but I felt compelled to check anyway. There weren't any. As I approached my house and stepped up to my door, I nearly tripped over the dog that bounded up to me..

"Jet!" I exclaimed, and fell forward, grabbing the door frame to keep myself from falling. He sat down on my doormat and looked up at me, smiling his doggy smile. His tail thumped happily.

"Well, I'm happy to see you, too," I said, and bent over to give him scritches behind his ears. "But we really need to find out who you belong to. C'mon. Let's head inside and I will text Babs. Maybe she'll finally tell me."

Jet's ears drooped, and he looked disappointed by my declaration.

"What, don't you want to go home? Surely you would rather be at home than with me. It's not like I have anything to feed you. I don't have any dog food!" I protested.

Jet spun around and faced the door, waiting eagerly for me to open it.

"Well, I guess we are going inside then," I said, and opened the door.

Jet darted inside and headed into the living room again, making himself at home on my couch.

"What the heck. I guess I'm making dinner for two," I said, heading over to my refrigerator to pull out chicken, rice, and black beans. I whipped up some quick cilantro-lime chicken with rice and beans, then cut up some of the chicken, mixed it with rice, and put it in a bowl.

"Buen Provecho! Enjoy!" I said, and served it up for the dog.

Jet just looked up at me and tilted his head before he sat down and daintily ate his dinner. I shrugged, served up my own portion, this time mixing in the black beans, then grabbed the open bottle of wine from the other night and poured myself a generous glass. I sat down and began to eat. Jet had already finished his dinner and moved to his favorite spot on the couch, where he curled into a ball. He wasn't sleeping but was watching me eat. He seemed to be trying to communicate something with his eyes, but I just wasn't picking up on the message.

"Look, kiddo, I'm sorry, but I'm no dog whisperer. I can't read your mind," I said. "You and I will eventually have to figure out who you belong to. I know that cats sometimes adopt people and not the other way around, but I've never heard of the same thing for dogs."

I took a sip of my wine, realizing that I was once again conversing with a dog—so basically, I was just talking to myself. My best bet for some real conversation was to call Penny; at least I would be speaking to another human being. I propped my phone on the decorative napkin holder in the island's center and cued up a video call. Penny answered on the third ring.

"Hey! What's up? Any updates on the investigation?"

"I'm not investigating!" I protested lamely.

"Move on from that nonsense and tell me what you know," Penny urged.

"Well, I found a series of emails between Arthur Odeon and Hilary Wen. It sounds like she was trying to sell something belonging to the association on Claire's List. Odeon must have discovered her classified ad and contacted her via an obscure screen name. At first, he pretended to be an interested buyer, but then he ultimately called her out directly."

"What was she trying to sell?" Penny sounded excited.

"I don't really know. The emails only showed snippets of the message conversations. You had to click on the '*read more*' link to see the rest, but when I clicked on it, the post and its messages had expired," I explained.

"What could she possibly have been selling on Claire's List, and why didn't Odeon go straight to the police once he found out about it?" Penny asked.

"I don't know. However, they repeated a few words, 'proof' was one . . . and, strange as it *seems,* 'paranormal' was another. I couldn't make heads or tails of it. That's why I messaged Hilary; I needed more information," I stated.

"You did what?!" Penny exclaimed.

I explained to Penny how I had seen a message containing the phrase "he's a dragon" and took advantage of that specific detail to send Hilary Wen's seller profile a message. "But don't worry," I added. "I used my email address and handle from college, which I haven't used in years."

"Are you sure there isn't any way she can trace it back to you?" Penny asked, fear creeping into her voice. I heard a whimper from the direction of the couch and turned to see Jet, apparently listening to our conversation. His whimper seemed to echo Penny's concerns.

"Was that Jet?" she asked.

"Yes, I can't seem to shake the pup. He keeps coming back here," I said, turning the camera in his direction.

"I'm kind of glad about that; at least you have a dog to help protect you and let you know if there are strangers at your house. This whole disappearance situation is making me nervous," Penny said, relief washing over her face.

"Well, it can't last forever; he has to belong to somebody," I said.

"I'm sure you'll sort it out. Back to my question. Are you sure that she won't know that it was you who sent the message?" Penny persisted.

"I'm not sure, but I think it's unlikely. I haven't really used that email address for anything but shopping online. It's where all my junk mail and advertisements go. I don't use any chat rooms with that screen name, and I doubt she would connect me with a 1991 Eddie Bauer edition Ford Bronco. I've never owned that model; it was my dad's," I said, trying to convince myself, as well.

"Still, that was a pretty big risk that you took. What if Hilary finds out it was you? You could be out of a job or worse!" Penny urged, fear creeping back into her voice.

"I doubt it, but I'll be careful. I promise," I said, and held my pinky up toward the phone. She mirrored my gesture in a virtual pinky promise.

We changed subjects for a bit; mainly, Penny cooed over Jet and what an adorable dog he was, but then she had to hop off the call to head to her yoga class. Putting my phone down on the counter, I curled up with Jet on the sofa and flicked on the TV. I scrolled through the guide until I found the listing for the movie, *Murder on the Orient Express.*

"Well, if you can't beat 'em, join 'em, right Jet?" I joked. "I think we could learn a lesson or two from Monsieur Hercule Poirot. He doesn't run around getting into trouble like Nancy Drew; he just uses his little gray cells and solves crimes from the comfort of his armchair."

Jet nudged my hand with his nose. I couldn't tell if he agreed with me or was trying to get me to scritch him behind his ears. I guess it was finally time to admit to myself that I really was doing this investigation thing.

Jet and I watched the movie, and then I went up to bed. I was exhausted. My dinner and the glass of wine had staved off the worst of my headache and worry, but I could still feel the nest of knots tightening in my stomach. I brushed my teeth, put on some comfy flannel pajama pants and an old novelty T-shirt, took some melatonin, and slept.

In the morning, Jet again woke me up before my alarm clock, this time with the smell and feel of his warm breath on my face. His front paws were on the bed, and he was staring into my eyes. I raised my sleepy hand and gently pushed him away. Then I walked him down to the front door, just as I had done on Wednesday morning, and returned inside to get ready for my day.

After I showered, I found myself standing in the middle of my walk-in closet, trying to decide what to wear. I kicked myself for not having spent a little time last night planning my outfit for today's luncheon. I pressed the heels of my hands into my eyes; I could already feel a headache coming on.

"What a way to start a day," I muttered.

Eventually, I decided to dig out a white sheath dress I had once worn to my cousin's baby shower. It featured a square neckline in a classic cut that never seemed to go out of style, but it was probably about half a size too small for me. Nevertheless, I squeezed myself into it, grateful for the stretchy give of the fabric. I paired it with a black and white pinstripe blazer with three-quarter sleeves and flat black dress sandals. I even went the extra mile and put on makeup. I looked at myself in the mirror.

This will have to do, I thought. I hoped I wasn't setting people's expectations too high; I never wore makeup if I could help it.

I was hungry and still very tired, but I hesitated to grab a cup of coffee or eat breakfast before leaving the house, convinced that I would spill something on this white get-up. I scolded myself again for not eating breakfast before I showered and dressed. Well, it was too late now; I would surely smudge my makeup if I tried to take this dress off. I looked longingly at the French press on the stove.

You'll be fine, you can make it until lunch, I told myself. My stomach growled in protest while simultaneously tying the anxiety knots up a little tighter.

I sighed heavily and hoisted my messenger bag onto my left shoulder, instead of slinging it over cross-body style, as I usually did. I didn't want to wrinkle my dress. I looked at the temperature for the day on my phone. Fortunately, it was cool enough right now that I didn't think I would break into sweat and ruin my outfit. Still, ridiculously, I debated taking my car the short distance to work just so that I could have air conditioning. Shaking my head, I pressed on and headed toward the clubhouse.

CHAPTER THIRTEEN

After the short walk to work, I pulled open the front door and sighed with relief as I stepped into the air conditioning. As I turned to head downstairs to the offices, my phone pinged. It was an unfamiliar notification sound, so I paused to check. It was from the Claire's List app that I had downloaded the night before. Hilary Wen had responded.

> Username: TheHilsRAlive
> Subject: The Dragon
> Dear BauerBronco91,
> Of course, the dragon is still availble. R u available to meet? Where r u located? Can we meet up to discuss this matter?"

I scurried downstairs as fast as possible to tell Babs about the message. When I entered the office, I stopped short. Hilary Wen was sitting in a visitor's chair in front of Bab's desk. I noticed that she slipped her phone into her purse just as she looked up at me.

"Good morning!" she said brightly. "I just thought I would stop by and see how you were doing. You look lovely, by the way. Are you headed to the luncheon today?"

I stood with my mouth open, unable to respond to her.

"She sure is," Babs responded on my behalf. "She's sitting at Alice's table."

"Oh, excellent! That is probably the best place for you to sit. Alice will make sure that you get to know everyone," Hilary said, smiling.

"Yeah . . ." I said, too surprised to form a decent response.

"Anyway. I was wondering if you have had a chance to catch up with Arty's emails and correspondence? He and I had been working on a project, and I was hoping to pick up with you where he and I left off."

"Project?" I asked stupidly, unsure if this was a trap or if she was just genuinely visiting as the board secretary.

"Yes, we were working on a historical archive, keeping track of information for the association," she said. I flicked my gaze to Babs, who was sitting behind Hilary. Babs shook her head no and shrugged, almost imperceptibly.

"Uh, no. I'm afraid I haven't had much chance to go through Arthur Odeon's emails. I've been pretty busy working on the board packet for next week and composing the IFB for the park restroom renovations. I hit the ground running, so to speak," I explained.

"Hmm. Okay, just reach out to me once you've had a chance to go through his emails. I really do want to pick that project back up, but it will be easier if you have the prior correspondence for reference. Once you have the background information, we can meet up to discuss this matter. See you at the luncheon." She smiled and headed back upstairs.

My heart was thudding so hard that I could hear it pounding in my ears. I felt like I would faint. I reached for Babs's desk to steady myself.

"She knows . . ." I whispered hoarsely.

"What? Are you okay?" Babs said, and came around her desk, taking my elbow to help me sit in the visitor's chair that Hilary had just vacated. I closed my eyes and took some steady, deep breaths, working deliberately to bring my racing heart rate back to normal. My dizzy spell abated, and I looked up at her.

It was then that I noticed what Babs was wearing. She had on a sleeveless yellow-orange turtleneck sweater and a red plaid skirt, with knee-high, yellow-orange stockings and reddish-brown Mary Janes. If her hair had been just a little longer, she would have looked exactly like an older, summery version of Velma from *Scooby-Doo*. Her ridiculously adorable outfit was enough to shake me out of my panic. I smiled to myself and shook my head.

"That was freaky," I said. "I think Hilary Wen just threatened me."

"How so?" Babs asked.

I explained the message I'd sent via Claire's List and the response I'd received just a few minutes ago.

"The phrasing is almost the same: 'We can meet up to discuss the matter,'" I explained.

"That's a common suggestion, it doesn't mean that she knows it was you who sent the message. Maybe it's just a turn of phrase that she favors," Babs said.

"I don't think so. Hilary was here fishing, trying to find out how much I knew. She wanted to know if I had been reading through Arthur Odeon's emails." I moved to press my palms into my eyes, but Babs grabbed my wrists gently and pulled my hands away.

"Don't do that; you'll mess up your make-up," she chided.

"Thanks," I said, putting my hands in my lap and wringing them tightly together.

"Okay, let's think about this logically. One: how would Hilary have figured out that it was you, and Two: why would she reveal that she knew that information? For all she knows, you haven't yet connected the Claire's List profile to her. Revealing herself to you would be risky," Babs rationalized.

"It's not risky, especially if she doesn't think I know it's her. She can fish to her heart's content and not risk being caught, mainly because she's hiding behind the anonymity of her screen name," I pointed out.

"You mean—just like you are?" Babs said. "You're doing the same thing, hiding behind your screen name and hoping she doesn't realize it's you. But somehow, you've convinced yourself that she has figured it out."

"What does she want? Does she really think that I will contact her and say, *Yes, I've gone through Arthur's email history; when can we meet up?*" I said, channeling every bit of snark that I possessed.

"If we go by your theory, then she doesn't need you to. Your reaction to her statement was enough. She read it on your face. She now knows that you know that she knows," Babs babbled.

I reached up again toward my face. Babs once again reached out, quick like lightning, and brushed my hands away from my face.

"Don't do that!" she cried.

"Sorry, I can't help it. It's a habit," I groaned.

"It's good that you are attending the luncheon today. It will at least ensure that you are surrounded by a ton of people. Nothing will happen to you while you are at the luncheon," Babs said reassuringly.

"Yeah, that's great, but what about when I have to walk home?" I protested.

"You should call the chief. Don't tell him about Hilary; just tell him you're afraid of the dark or something. Perhaps he can escort you home. I'm sure you would like that," Babs said with a tone that implied more than just personal safety. She winked at me and grinned like the Cheshire cat.

"No," I responded flatly, knowing that if I protested too much, she would take it as confirmation of her suspicions of a crush.

"For all you know, she could be the person behind Arty's disappearance, and you could be next!" she exclaimed.

"Thanks for that. You sure do know how to bolster a person's mood, make a person feel safe," I griped.

"I'm serious, and you should be too. You need to consider your safety. The information Hilary was selling on Claire's List is dangerous if it falls into the wrong hands," Babs said, her voice tinged with sincere worry.

"Information?" I asked, standing up and pointing a finger in her face. "How do you know it was information she was selling online?"

"I don't, I'm just guessing. Willow says nothing has gone missing from the association. I haven't noticed anything disappear, either. What else could she possibly be selling?" Babs reasoned.

"What kind of information? Member records?? Secrets about the association? Does the association have some dirty laundry that I haven't heard about?" I asked, nearly shouting. "What don't I know?"

"A lot," she answered meekly, but I knew by now that Babs doesn't do meek, so I immediately knew something was wrong.

"Like . . ." I said, gesturing to her to continue.

"I really can't say. It's not my place."

"Who can, and why is this information such a big secret from the general manager?!" I shouted.

"New, non-resident employees are typically told after their ninety-day eval, once the board can determine their credibility," she explained.

"Credibility? They did a background check on me, called all my references, even ran a credit check; what more proof of credibility do they need?" I asked, offended.

Babs stood there, mute, her campy outfit making her look even more like a still shot from a cartoon.

"Babs," I tried again, this time in my most placating voice, "I'm not just any employee; I am the general manager, and I am walking blindly into what feels like a trap. I need to know whatever it is you're not telling me."

"I don't know where to begin. Clive should be the one to do this," she said, still a little sheepish.

"Well, why don't you start with how you figured out that it's information Hilary Wen has been selling on Claire's List?" I directed.

"This should really be Clive's job," she mumbled.

"We can call him."

"No! No, he would be very upset by what you found out; we can't call him yet."

"'By what I found out'? I haven't *found* anything yet, at least not to my knowledge. Why don't you clue me in?" I said, snark rising in my voice.

"But you did. You found out that Hilary Wen was selling information about Clive. The dragon reference . . ." she paused and wrung her hands nervously, "it was about him."

"Clive is a dragon?" I asked, referring to the clipped sentence in the email.

"Yes," she said.

I puzzled over some of the other odd things I'd noticed in the emails; the word *paranormal* had certainly jumped out at me. "Are you trying to tell me that he is literally a dragon?"

"Yes," she said quietly.

"Jinkies Velma, I guess we solved it! Should I call Mystery, Inc.?" I quipped. I was not prepared to believe this nonsense. There had to be another explanation.

"Quit it, Kat. I'm serious," Babs said, reviving her usually spicy personality.

"Fine, you're serious then. Say I believe you, and Hilary Wen was selling some information about Clive being a dragon online; what exactly does that mean? Is that like the title of some high leader in a secret group? Kind of like the Worshipful Master of the Masonic Lodge?" I asked.

"No, it's more literal than that. That's the thing about Blackwater Lake: it's a special place for special people. It's a place where people can be themselves, which is why the board is so particular about checking out the credibility of new employees before divulging the details."

"Literal? A literal dragon? How can that be? I met him, rode in a car with him, and shook his hand. He doesn't seem much like a dragon to me," I said.

"Haven't you noticed how he wears layers of clothing—sweaters, shirts, and vests—even when it's ninety degrees outside?" Babs asked.

"Yes . . ."

"I noticed that after your tour, your hair was limp and you were covered in sweat. I'm guessing that Clive didn't turn on the air conditioning in his car?" she reminded me.

"So . . . what? You're trying to tell me he is cold-blooded, like a dragon?" I asked.

"Yes." She held her shoulders back and her head high to emphasize her sincerity.

"This is ridiculous. Next, you will tell me that his house is filled with gold and jewels and that he is the descendant of Smaug," I growled.

"Not gold and jewels, but rather books."

"Books? I'm not tracking; what do books have to do with a dragon?" I asked.

"He's not your typical dragon; instead of hoarding gold and jewels, he prefers to hoard books. It was why he was exiled from his clan and came here to live," Babs stated.

"He's a dragon who hoards books instead of gold and came here because he was exiled from the dragon community?" I repeated, still unable to truly comprehend what I was hearing.

"Like I said, this is a special community for special people," she answered, as if that explained everything.

"So, if I'm following this conversation, you're telling me that Hilary Wen found out that Clive was a real live dragon of some sort, and she sold this and other information about Blackwater Lake's 'special people' on the internet. She just put it out there on Claire's List, the way you would sell a used car?" I said incredulously.

"Yes, but honestly, I think using Claire's List was very stupid. It's no wonder that Arty caught her in the act," Babs said.

"Assuming I believe you that Clive is some sort of dragon, what other types of 'special people' are living here? What about you? What about Hilary?" I asked.

"I'm not all that special," Babs said dismissively, though I didn't believe her. "Hilary, however, is descended from the Huli Jing. I'm not totally familiar with her background, but from what I understand, she is not pure Huli Jing; she's got some nymph or something in her bloodlines. I've often heard her complaining about how she thinks people treat her unfairly because of her lineage."

"I have never heard of a Huli Jing. What is that?"

"They are paranormal shapeshifting foxes from Chinese mythology. They are almost always women, and they use the power of illusion to deceive people."

"Illusion? You mean like whatever happened to the minutes to hide the nonsense that Odeon was writing when he was slowly spiraling into insanity?" I could totally empathize with the feeling of losing one's grip on reality.

"Yes, that type of illusion," Babs answered.

"If you knew she could create illusions, why didn't you suspect her? Report her to the chief or Detective Daniels when we discovered the concealed minutes?" I asked.

"Because—" She paused. "Frankly, she's just not that good. Even Hilary herself lamented that her powers were limited. I didn't think it could have been her. Plus, she's a board member; I couldn't imagine a board member putting everything we have worked for at risk. I'm still not sure what her motive would have been."

I reached up again to press the heel of my palms against my eyes; this time, she didn't try to stop me.

"This is all too much; I don't know what to do with this information. Does the chief know that Clive is a dragon?" I asked.

"Yes, most people know."

"I didn't know!" I said emphatically. "I just can't imagine it. Does he turn into a dragon? Like with scales and a tail?"

"He is always a dragon; his human form is his glamour, a disguise," Babs explained. I shook my head, still not able to wrap my mind around the physics of it all. The type of dragon that I could imagine would never fit into a car, glamour or no glamour.

"And Hilary Wen believed that this information was valuable, that someone would buy it? What could they do with it if they had this information? Would anyone believe them?" I scoffed.

"There's a black market for information on the paranormal. If it falls into the wrong hands, then the protections that this community provides are jeopardized. We're lucky that Arty caught onto her when he did; she could have ruined everything," Babs said.

I wanted to press her again about what type of 'special person' she was, seeing as she had evaded answering my previous question, but I wasn't sure I could take any more wild news.

Odeon had tried to stop Hilary from sharing the secrets of this town, and something had caused him to disappear. Whatever "it" was, Hilary had taken six months to finally pull it off, and she somehow drove Arthur insane in the process. I was confused by all of this, and I was having a very hard time processing it all—this new and unfathomable information about the town and its people, as well as the mystery of Arty's disappearance.

"What do I do now?" I asked.

"You pretend. Behave as if you don't know anything about it. You need to go to the luncheon today. It will look suspicious if you don't go, and Hilary will suspect you even more," Babs urged.

"Babs, she already suspects me. That was the point of her showing up here earlier," I protested.

"Yes, but she's still not sure that you have enough proof to expose her. Otherwise, she would have done more than threaten you," Babs said.

"So, you suggest I just pretend that all is well? Pretend that I don't know anything about 'special people.' I can't do that!" I cried. "I will look at every person at that luncheon and wonder about their special abilities."

"You can't tell anyone that you know. Not for another eighty-five-and-a-half days, at least!" Babs declared.

"That will be a little difficult when I report all this to the chief and Detective Daniels," I said, reaching to pick up her phone.

"You're not listening!" Babs exclaimed.

"I am listening, but I disagree. I can't hide this information. I need to tell the chief about Hilary Wen. Give me one good reason why I shouldn't!" I taunted her with the receiver in my hand.

"I don't have one; it's just a gut feeling. At the very least, I think you should wait until after the luncheon. Act natural and dispel Hilary's suspicions. She'll be anticipating that you'll call them right now. She's probably preparing to run—or at least destroy all the evidence. You must convince her that she's still getting away with it; put her mind at ease."

"That doesn't make any sense. The more time I give Hilary, the more time she has to plan her escape and ditch all the evidence," I said.

"Whatever. I just want you to be safe, but you do what you believe necessary," Babs said. She spun around and left the office to head upstairs. The phone in my hand started beeping with the off-the-hook tone, and I slammed it back down on the cradle.

"What the flying monkeys!" I exclaimed.

I sighed heavily and headed down the hall to the office's single-stall restroom, make-up kit in hand. The harsh white LED lights confirmed that, sure enough, I had smeared all my eye shadow off. I touched up my face and then washed the eye shadow residue from my palms, wishing that I could splash some water on my newly made-up face to refresh myself.

I had two choices: I could go into my office, pick up the phone, call the chief, and tell him everything that I know. Or I could go to the luncheon and pretend like nothing had happened. I looked myself in the eye via the mirror.

"Do you have enough evidence to make it stick? What if you are wrong, and you accuse an innocent person?" I asked myself out loud.

That settled it for me. I was nervous and afraid of being the next victim, but I didn't want to falsely accuse someone. I had just started this job and hadn't even been here a week; far be it from me to throw away this career opportunity based on some spurious suspicions. I wasn't even supposed to be investigating; that wasn't my job. I was the general manager, not Nancy Drew.

I straightened my dress and blazer and stepped out of the bathroom. Babs was sitting back at her desk; she clacked away at her keyboard and refused to look up at me. With my messenger bag slung over my shoulder, I breezed past her desk and headed into my office.

I killed time for the next few hours. I read emails unrelated to Hilary Wen, wrote memos, and prepared my notes for next week's board meeting. Around eleven a.m., Babs came into my office and placed a map of the waterfront on my desk. It was labeled "Concert" and had handwritten notations referencing the barge location for the band, security post positions, boat tie-up spots, and picnic tables.

"What's this?" I asked.

"It's the set-up plan for tomorrow's concert; Noah dropped it off earlier. He wants to know if you approve," Babs said coolly, still miffed, I assumed, by our previous conversation.

"Why didn't he just bring it in and show it to me himself?" I asked.

"I told him you were busy," she said flatly.

"Why would you do that?" I asked, shock resonating in my voice. "You should have at least checked to see if I actually was busy before shooing him away."

"Is the map approved or not?" Babs asked.

"Is it different from what we've done in the past? How many security officers are on staff tomorrow? What are the rules for members and guests who wish to watch the concert?" I asked, only blurting out a few of the millions of questions running through my head.

"It's the same. Four off-duty officers are working on the detail. Members may enjoy and watch the concert from land, water, or boat. Alcohol is allowed, but driving while intoxicated is not, even on the boats," Babs said, listing off the answers.

"Okay then, well, I approve the map. Please let Noah know, since you chased him away before I could speak with him," I said, bitterly.

"Fine," Babs answered. She scooped up the map and headed back out of my office. I resisted the urge to press the heels of my hands into my eyes again.

A half-hour later, I decided to head up to the Shopette. I figured my best bet for now was to head to the luncheon with Alice. At least she could break the ice and introduce me to all of the players. What was it that Babs had called them—a flock of hens? That couldn't be a good sign. I was definitely better off going to this luncheon with an ally.

I found Alice preparing to lock up the Shopette. She had pulled shut the bi-fold French doors that served as the security barrier and was latching them into place. As promised, she wore white slacks and her mother's "vintage" nineties red Chanel blazer. She looked lovely, like a young Katherine Hepburn, and I wondered just how old she was. She turned her key in the lock and spun around to face me.

"Wow! That's a great outfit," she said, complimenting me before I had a chance to do the same. She reached up and, with a delicate finger, wiped something away from my left eye. "Your makeup was smudged," she said, shrugging.

"Thanks." I smiled.

"C'mon, let's go in early. You can grab a mint julep from the bar before they are all gone," she said, tugging on my elbow.

"Mint-juleps. Haven't had one of those before. In fact, I've only ever heard of them in *The Great Gatsby*."

"It's a tradition, a sendoff to summer. Technically, the club pays for one complimentary drink per person, but in reality, it's a free-for-all. Most of us ladies know at least one member who doesn't drink and will use their name as an excuse to get a second glass. More often than not, the same non-drinker's name is invoked several times throughout the afternoon." Alice giggled as she explained.

"I'm game. Far be it from me to snub tradition." I grinned. We wove our way through the slowly growing crowd of women to one of the bars set up along the windowed wall, each grabbing a cocktail glass off the table. Alice paused to chat with the bartender. He was a younger Black man, probably about Alice's age, with carved features, a bald head, and a lean build. His long-sleeved black uniform shirt and black pants gave him a debonaire look.

"Trent, this is our new boss, Kat. Kat, this is Trent, a server and bartender for The Roanoke. He always works this event; the ladies love him and tip him well," Alice said, winking at him.

"Nice to meet you, ma'am," Trent said to me. Then, grinning widely, he leaned in toward Alice and said, conspiratorially, "Thanks for blabbing that, Lis. It's a trade secret; you're not supposed to tell anyone."

She giggled, swatted him playfully with her hand, then fished a five-dollar bill out of one of her blazer pockets and dropped it into the vase that was serving as the tip jar. Trent winked at her, and she waved back, taking my elbow and towing me out onto the deck.

"I didn't think to bring any cash to tip the servers. I'll have to make it up to Trent," I said, bashfully.

"Don't worry about it; he'll do just fine today. Besides, there was no way you could have known all the etiquette for this event," she said reassuringly. I felt a little embarrassed that this young employee, nearly half my age, had to serve as my social ambassador. Still, I was also very relieved to have Alice on my side.

It was now noon, and the crowd was at capacity. Women of all ages milled around the bars, the high-top tables, and the deck. Everyone wore some variation of white; most paired pants or a skirt with a different colored blouse or jacket, but some had gone all-in. One older woman wore a dazzling sequined white jumpsuit with a halter-style cowl neckline. Her white sandals, pedicure, and French tip manicure tied it all together in an over-the-top way. I found myself staring; even her hair was a perfect shade of white. She looked almost swanlike. She must have been in her sixties, but she was as fit and as gorgeous as any of the younger women, including Jessica, with whom she was talking.

"That would be Robin Odeon," Alice said when she caught the direction of my stare.

"But . . . she's quite a bit older than Jessica. I thought they were best friends," I stammered.

"They are," Alice said, shrugging. "Come over here; I want to introduce you to my mother." She led the way to a glamorous older woman chatting with a group of ladies. Her mother wore a tailored white pantsuit with a sapphire blue blouse under her jacket. Her rose gold accessories—including a beautiful red, white, and blue cloisonne bracelet—accented her outfit perfectly, and her silver-white pointed-toe shoes dressed the outfit up to just the right level. It was no wonder that Alice was willing to wear her mother's hand-me-downs. Her mother had style.

"Mom, this is Katherine Normand, the new general manager. Kat, this is my mother, Delia French."

I extended my hand, and Delia took it and embraced it with both of hers. She smiled genuinely and with warmth.

"Welcome!" she said. "I'm so glad you could join us today. Let me introduce you to the rest of the elders."

Delia turned back to the other four women with whom she was talking, explaining that they were only called the "elders" because they were all past presidents and they all had at least one daughter in the Ladies Auxiliary of Blackwater Lake, affectionately known as the LAX. They were also the ones who funded most of the events and charitable activities. Their donations were what kept the service club going. They were lively women, and I relaxed as we chatted. The mint julep I was sipping may have also helped to ease some of my nerves.

CHAPTER FOURTEEN

A chime rang out, and Alice again grabbed me by the elbow, pulling me inside. Her mother chided her for being so handsy, but I didn't mind. I was grateful for Alice's energy, cheer, and kindness. Alice and I made our way to one of the tables up at the front of the room, right next to that of the lady elders.

When we pulled out our chairs to sit down, I nearly tripped over my sandals. Hilary Wen, Jessica Cheverie, and Robin Odeon sat at the table. The three women whom I least wanted to see. Alice caught me by the elbow she was still holding and kept me from toppling facedown into the summer strawberry, feta, and mint salad plated on the table at my seat. I put on a smile and forced myself to sit down. Alice pretended that I didn't know anyone and took the liberty of making introductions.

"This is the head table; we're all officers of the LAX," she explained. "Jessica is president, Robin is the treasurer, and Hilary is the secretary."

"You're the secretary for the LAX as well as the board?" I asked, to be conversational.

"Of course, it's what I'm good at. I write well and I'm well-organized," Hilary bragged.

"Right, of course you are," I said, matching her snotty tone.

Jessica glared at me from across the table, but I couldn't comprehend the subliminal messages she was trying to send me. She stabbed inelegantly at a strawberry on her plate. I noticed she hadn't even bothered to put the vinaigrette dressing on her salad. *What a waste*, I thought as I poured the delicious-smelling pink dressing onto my own greens. Ignoring her, I turned my attention back to Hilary.

"So, Hilary," I prompted, "what project were you and Arthur Odeon working on before he disappeared?" I tried to sound inquisitive and not nosy.

"You were working on a project with Arty?" Robin asked Hilary in surprise. "You never mentioned it to me."

"It was an association matter; I didn't want to discuss it," Hilary told Robin in a slightly annoyed tone.

"I would be very curious to know what it was; perhaps I can help bring it to fruition," I interjected.

"Like I said earlier," Hilary retorted, "it would be a lot easier to bring you up to speed once you have had a chance to go through Odeon's emails and read the background correspondence."

"Frankly, Hilary, I don't think I will have the time to go through all of Odeon's emails. I've barely had time to eat lunch at work until today," I said, raising my glass in salute to the delicious-looking entrée that was now replacing the salad at some of the other tables.

"Well, it can wait then," Hilary said, pasting on her fake smile again.

"I would like to know what the project was too," Robin said, oblivious of the tension between Hilary and me. "I thought you didn't like Arty, Hils?"

"Like I said, it's really nothing of consequence," Hilary said crisply.

Jessica was taking in the conversation and had been uncharacteristically silent the whole time. She sat straight as a rail and daintily finished her salad, but her eyes pinged back and forth between me and Hilary. I could feel her gaze and almost hear the gears turning in her head. I knew that for all her hoity-toity, pretentious attitude, she was not an idiot; after all, she was a paralegal working on passing the bar to become a lawyer. She was undoubtedly already picking up on the clues of the conversation and crafting the story in her head. I needed to change the subject.

Thankfully, the chimes rang out again, and Ruth, one of the elders, stepped up to the lectern.

"Good afternoon, ladies, and welcome to our annual end-of-summer luncheon. You are all looking spectacular today. Let's get a little business out of the way while the servers bring around our lunch entrée. By the way, I heard that the dessert is your choice of either strawberry or chocolate cheesecake, so be sure not to fill up on cocktails!" The room filled with polite laughter at what appeared to be a well-used joke.

The business part of the LAX meeting was short. There was the approval of the minutes, a vote about which project to fund, and a discussion about the theme for the spring gala. Once the business was concluded, everyone returned to their seats and continued to enjoy their lunch of citrus rosemary chicken or fish. I was grateful for the interlude because it redirected the conversation at the table.

Shortly after the meeting, Alice hopped up and buzzed over to the bar counter; somehow, she had wrangled up a tray of a half dozen mint juleps and she brought them back to the table. Trailing behind her was a tall woman dressed in a simple white cotton strappy sundress, its scalloped hem embellished with wavy blue abstract embroidery. She was slender yet curvy, and the white dress complimented her caramel skin, naturally curly hair, and brown eyes. She was stunning. The way she moved gave off a feeling of fluidity, and I wondered what type of "special person" she was.

"Kat, this is my good friend Hennah," said Alice.

Hennah passed around the drinks, then took one of the empty seats and joined us at the table. A server came by and immediately switched out the chicken for the fish without Hennah even needing to ask. I raised an eyebrow in curiosity.

"I'm a pescatarian," Hennah explained, shrugging.

"I'm so sorry; I didn't mean to stare. It's very nice to meet you," I said, trying to recover some courtesy.

"No worries," Hennah said. She spoke languidly, reminding me of video clips of my parents' generation; they had both been hippies when they were young.

"Hennah is an instructor for the association—well, not for the HOA, but contracted by the HOA," Alice rambled. "She teaches yoga, Zumba, water aerobics, trapeze, hot yoga . . ."

Hennah reached out a hand and placed it on her friend's arm.

"I think she gets it, my dear," Hennah said quietly.

"Oh," Alice said, and giggled sheepishly.

"So, do you live in the Lake?" I asked, trying to make small talk. The entire table went dead silent. Everyone stopped what they were doing mid-bite or sip.

"I mean here, within the association," I clarified. Everyone visibly relaxed and resumed their meal; I wondered what my faux pas had been. Perhaps people didn't like to refer to the community as "the Lake." I filed that information away for later.

"Yes, I do. I love it here. I understand they have put you up in the A-frame house nearby. How do you like it?" she asked, picking up the thread of small talk as if the awkwardness had never happened.

"It's perfect. It's exactly what I would have chosen for a lake-front house if I was building one. There's just one thing that bothers me," I said.

"What's that?" Alice asked.

"The second bedroom, the one on the first floor across from the bathroom/laundry room area," I explained. "It's been repainted, but poorly, and you can tell that someone once spent a great deal of time painting a vintage style mural from the early age of flight."

"You mean like when Neil Armstrong walked on the moon?" Alice asked.

"No, you idiot, she means like when the Wright Brothers flew," Jessica chided. It was the first time she had spoken since Hennah had joined the table.

"Of course. I knew that!" Alice exclaimed.

"Even though it's been painted over, I can tell it was originally made with love. There are bi-planes, hot air balloons, dirigibles, and some of the more novel aircraft from very early on," I continued, thrilled to finally have an opportunity to ask about it. "Do any of you know who may have painted it?"

"All I know is that an older couple lived in that house for decades. When they passed away, they bequeathed it to the HOA with the terms that it could only be used to house the general manager if he or she should choose to live there," Hilary said.

"I heard that they had a son who had passed away, but I'm not sure when that happened or how old he was at the time," Jessica added.

"I'm almost inclined to hire someone to fix the mural; it would feel less creepy than having it faintly painted over. Other than that, though, I love the house and enjoy working here," I said, trying to lighten the mood.

"And we're so glad you accepted the job," Hilary said with obvious insincerity. Hennah was the only one who seemed to pick up on it, and she quickly changed the subject.

The conversation moved on to other topics, and it never circled back around to a point where I could grill Hilary or Robin on what else they might know about Arty's disappearance. Having met Robin, I was now reasonably confident she had nothing to do with the case. She was too wrapped up in herself and her own life to hold a grudge against someone else for very long. She also seemed quite content with her new beau. She took any and every opportunity to bring her new relationship up in the conversation.

The luncheon concluded with a brief ritual that involved the LAX pledge and a discussion of the schedule for the next few weeks. People mingled around afterward, networking and socializing for another half hour. All in all, it was a good event. I met a handful of new people, thanks to Alice, and some seemed like they would actually be good connections. Alice and I parted ways in the main lobby; she returned to re-open the Shopette, and I headed downstairs. I was kicking myself for not having thought to bring a change of clothes for the afternoon, but I wanted to get back to the office and didn't feel like I had time to take the short walk home.

Back in the office, Babs was chatting on the phone with a community member. They were discussing the upcoming concert as well as other recent events. I smiled and waved to her, but she didn't wave back. I wondered just how long she would be mad at me for disagreeing about how to handle the situation with Odeon's disappearance. After all, I hadn't actually called the chief; instead, I had gone to the luncheon and pretended that everything was normal . . . sort of.

Hilary Wen was clearly hiding something. Her attitude toward me had changed from formal, polite, and professional to wary and snarky. Jessica had been acting strangely as well, although I certainly didn't know why. As far as I knew, she was not involved in the case. She was just the snobbish blond bombshell who was dating Jay Baxter, the Blackwater chief of police.

Whoa there, bitter much? I said to myself as I sat down at my desk.

I pulled my phone out of my messenger bag and checked it. I had left it in my office during lunch, wanting to be unencumbered; Babs knew where to find me if something came up. I had two new messages from the Claire's List app. With my heart racing, I opened them.

The first one was sent shortly after the luncheon and read:

Username: TheHilsRAlive
Subject: Re: The Dragon
Kat. Lets meet. Youe obviously know more than u are letting on.

The second message read:
Username: TheHilsRAlive
Subject: Re: Re: The Dragon

South Beach, 10 p.m.

That was ominous. Clearly, Hilary hadn't bought my ignorance act. Then again, I hadn't been very subtle when I asked her about her special project. Dang it! I wasn't very good at this investigation stuff. Perhaps I had been right the first time and should have called Chief Baxter. I reread the messages. *Is there enough evidence for me to make a phone call to him?*

"Not really," I said out loud to myself. I had been the one to start the conversation in the app, and now I really wished I hadn't. I had never responded to Hilary's first email, but that didn't really matter. Without the context of our earlier face-to-face conversations, it appeared this was just a continuation of my inquiry into the dragon. There wasn't really anything for the chief or Detective Daniels to go on except the possibility of Hilary Wen selling information illicitly on the internet.

Despite what Babs had said, I had a hard time believing that everyone in this town thought that Clive was a dragon or that there was enough information about the "special people" who lived here to sell online for any profit. All of it was just too far-fetched. A dragon who hoards books instead of treasure, and who can glamour himself into a human? It was far more likely that Hilary had stolen something of value and was trying to sell it on the internet. Perhaps it wasn't something that belonged to the association, but instead to one or more of the community members. That certainly seemed a more likely scenario than the one about the dragon. I put my phone back on my desk and glanced at the time. It was nearly two o'clock. I wasn't sure how I would while away the next eight hours until the proposed meetup with Hilary, but I would have to find a way to get by. Anyway, I was fairly certain that I wasn't going to go to South Beach.

* * *

Somehow, the time passed faster than expected. Several women I'd met at the luncheon came down to make requests and pitch proposals that they had hoped to share with me at the event. They talked animatedly and rattled off their well-thought-out suggestions for improvements to the amenities, programs, or the community in general. I spent about half an hour with each of them in turn. Babs expertly queued them out in the reception area and admitted them individually. None of them seemed perturbed at waiting; they seemed to enjoy the extra time they spent chatting with their friends. Between those conversations and the remaining preparations for the concert on Friday, I was kept busy until five p.m.

Babs came into my office right before closing and grabbed my planner off of my desk. She flipped through it, making a few new notations and crossing out one or two items, then tossed the planner back on my desk without ceremony, clasped her hands behind her, and stared at me. She really did look like an older version of Velma from Scooby Doo.

"What?" I blurted out.

"Jet is here. He's out in the reception room. I think you should take him home with you tonight," Babs said.

"What? No! Who does that dog belong to anyway? Doesn't he have a family?" I protested.

"He can stay with you again tonight; no one will miss the poor kid anyway," she said sadly.

"Are you saying that he doesn't actually have a home? He's a stray?" I asked.

"Not a stray, per se. A lot of us care about him very much, but he seems to have taken a shine to you more than most of us. You might actually get him to come out of his shell a little bit. Just take him home with you tonight. He can walk you home and see that you are safe, and he will alert you to potential intruders."

"Weren't you the one who said he's just a pup? What could he really do to protect me? And I still don't have any dog food," I protested.

"He'll eat whatever you eat. He doesn't need any special food. In fact, he doesn't much care for dog food. He's a bit of a picky eater, for a dog," she said.

"Fine. I will take Jet home with me, but you must give me more information about his status tomorrow. I can't just keep a stray dog in my home. I'm not sure if the association even allows me to have pets in that house!" I argued.

"Whatever. I'll just feel better knowing that you have him with you. He may be young, but his hearing and his sense of smell are excellent." With that, she spun around and headed out my office door in a blur of orange.

I pressed the heels of my hands to my eyes once more, feeling another stress headache coming on and not caring one iota about the condition of my makeup. I snatched up my messenger bag, slung it across my body, grabbed my cellphone, and headed to the reception area. Jet was sitting curled up with his front legs crossed on one of the visitors' chairs. He perked up when he saw me come out of my office. I looked around and realized that Babs had already left for the day.

"Well, shall we go?" I asked the pup.

Without waiting for a response, I locked up my office and the main reception area and headed back upstairs with Jet at my heels. As I reached the lobby, I once again ran right into Jessica, literally. She seemed to have been pacing the floor as if waiting for someone. She and I stepped back out of each other's personal space, and it was then that I realized something was off. I hadn't heard the tell-tale click-clack of her fancy shoes on the floor. I glanced down and realized that she had removed her stiletto heels and now held them in her left hand. *Just how long has she been pacing the lobby?* I asked myself.

"What's going on?" I asked suspiciously.

"I was just about to ask you the same question," Jessica said.

"I'm headed home. Why are you pacing around up here . . . without your shoes on?"

"My feet were killing me," Jessica said, answering only part of the question. Jet came around beside me and sat at my feet. He looked up at Jessica quizzically but didn't wag his tail.

"Is that Jet?" she asked.

"Of course not, it's the Royal Canin dog," I snarked. She rolled her eyes at me.

"Are you taking him home with you?" she asked.

"That's the plan. Babs seems to think it's a good idea for some reason," I said.

"It is," Jessica answered cryptically. "He's a good pup; he'll smell or hear trouble long before you see it. He'll alert you if there is a problem."

"What trouble? Wait . . . are you worried about me?" I asked, confused.

"Not in the least," she said. "I have to meet up with a client in the lounge." She padded off toward the bar on bare feet.

"Put your shoes back on!" I called.

Jet and I headed out of the clubhouse and up the trail to my house. He stayed close to me the entire time—never ventured ahead or stopped to sniff something interesting, as he was wont to do. Strangely, his proximity to me made me more nervous rather than less. I began to place more stock in the concerns that Babs had expressed, and I wondered if I really was at risk from Hilary.

Why didn't I just call the chief? I chided myself.

It wasn't too late to do so. I could call him once I got back to the house. Once again, my mind raced through the many reasons supporting both sides of the argument, but ultimately, not calling him won out. I still only had circumstantial evidence. There wasn't anything that the police could do about it. Plus, I didn't want the chief putting a protective detail on my house like I was a V.I.P. I could just picture it: four days into my new job I get assigned my own secret service bodyguard; it would be gossip fodder for weeks.

Jet and I arrived at the house, and he leaped onto the porch, sniffing back and forth along the deck and in front of the door. I let him sniff away and stayed down on the gravel path. When he finished, he sat on the door mat, barked once, and wagged his tail. I felt sure that he was signaling that it was safe to go into the house.

"All clear, huh?" I probed. He barked again, and his tail thumped happily against the door.

"All right then, what would you like for dinner? Bark once for chicken alfredo or twice for grilled ham and cheese sandwiches," I asked.

He tilted his head as if contemplating the question and then barked twice.

"Grilled ham and cheese sandwiches it is!" I replied.

I unlocked the door and Jet dashed into the house ahead of me, sniffing all the while. Seemingly satisfied that no boogeymen were present, he took up his usual place on the sofa. I went to the kitchen, took out the skillet and all the sandwich fixings, grilled two ham and cheese sandwiches to golden perfection, and steamed some frozen green beans in the microwave.

I cut up Jet's sandwich and vegetables to make it easier for him to eat, and he hopped off the couch to eat his dinner off the plate at my feet. I sat down at the island and ate my dinner as well.

"Should I try and meet up with Hilary tonight?" I asked Jet, in between bites of cheesy goodness. He let out a low growl; clearly, he was not in favor of that idea.

"But what if I don't? Won't she find another way to get to me? At least if I go there tonight, I know I'm walking into a trap. I could be prepared," I said, talking more to myself than to the dog. Jet whined in response.

"What if you come with me?" I asked him, once again not sure why I was conversing with a dog. Jet whined once more; he didn't like that idea either.

"Fine," I said, and went back to finishing my dinner.

After dinner, Jet and I sat on the couch and watched a few episodes of the latest Star Trek series. Between the move and the new job, I had fallen behind and I needed to catch up. I remembered watching *Star Trek: The Next Generation* when I was a kid and having to schedule my school nights around new episodes. If I missed it, then I had to wait for it to air on a re-run. *Thank goodness for modern-day streaming options,* I thought.

The house was feeling a little too warm and stuffy; it was slightly uncomfortable. I got off the couch and opened the sliding glass door, looking out onto the lake. It was a beautiful night. The sun was nearly set, the moon had not yet risen, and I could hear the waves lapping up against the shoreline bulkhead. I returned to the couch and sprawled out again, pulling the throw blanket over myself. Jet had watched me open the sliding glass door. He sniffed the air briefly and then curled up at my feet.

The dog was adorable, and instinctively, I felt the urge to hug and protect him. Once again, I couldn't imagine why anyone would abandon this dog. How had no one inquired about him over the past week? Surely, there was someone who was missing him and looking for him.

I reached down toward my feet and scratched him behind the ears. Jet opened one eye, looked at me, and then went right back to sleep. He wasn't interested in being social, just sleeping. I clicked off the television and laid my head on the throw pillow. My eyes grew heavy, and I drifted off to sleep.

CHAPTER FIFTEEN

I woke to Jet barking near the open sliding glass door. It felt like I had only been asleep for a few minutes, but it must have been hours. I looked over at the clock on the TV box and saw it was just after ten p.m. It was still warm outside, but I felt a chill, so I wrapped the throw blanket around my shoulders as I walked over to where Jet stood and tried to peer out the screen. Fortunately, I hadn't turned the lights on earlier this evening, so it was dark enough to allow my night vision to acclimate to the night landscape.

"What are you barking at?" I asked the dog, not really expecting an answer. He let out an ominous low growl.

"Well, I don't like the sound of that," I said, and stared out into the darkness toward the lake, trying to sense or see what Jet perceived.

Suddenly, a slightly dizzying sensation came over me, and I closed my eyes briefly. When I opened them again, I saw Jet darting toward the dock as fast as his little feet could carry him.

"What the heck? Jet, come back!" I couldn't figure out how he had gotten out; the screen door was still shut. I threw the door open and ran down the hill after him, sliding the door closed behind me. I could hear him barking urgently, but it almost sounded like it was coming from behind me, near the house. I paused briefly and turned back around to see if he had doubled back, but the house was dark, and I couldn't see him, so I started again toward the water. When I got to the dock, he was sitting at the end of it, staring at the water. He wasn't moving, wasn't barking, wasn't growling. His tail didn't even swish in eagerness or apprehension. I approached the dock slowly, nervously. This felt wrong; it felt like a trap, but Jet would never lead me into a trap; I was sure of that.

"Jet," I said, just above a whisper; he didn't look back at me, just sat still.

"Jet!" I said a little louder, reaching down to put my hand on his head.

Someone grabbed my wrist and pulled me forward. I fell head over heels and landed on the bottom of a johnboat. A heavy, weighted net was thrown over me, and I heard the click of D-rings as they locked the net into place. I was stuck under the net, lying on my side in an uncomfortable position. I couldn't move, and for some reason I couldn't see. Everything around me was pitch black. At first, I thought some sort of tarp had been thrown over me to obscure my vision, but I could feel the weave of the net and the cooling night air against my skin. Someone or something had turned out the lights. I heard the propellers of an electric motor whir to life.

"Who's there?" I asked with more courage in my voice than I expected. There was only the sound of the electric motor in response.

I twisted under the net to get more comfortable while also trying to grope for the D-ring clips that I had heard earlier. If I could get them unclipped, then I could set myself free.

"Don't bother," a familiar female voice said. "You're not going to be able to undo them from where you are, not without your eyesight."

"Hilary? What the holy hockey pucks are you doing?" I yelled.

"That was supposed to be my question. Well, not the 'holy hockey pucks' part; who says that sort of thing anyway?" she quipped. "But just what did you think you were doing by digging into Arty's disappearance?"

"I wasn't digging into anything," I retorted, still not wanting to admit to her that I was investigating.

"You certainly were. You and your little band of friends, that is," she said snidely.

"Hilary, I have been here all of four days; I haven't had time to recruit *a band of friends*," I said, trying to distract her as I continued to grope around in the dark. It wasn't that I was blind; it was more like all the light had been sucked out from the immediate area around me. I could see a dim glow just beyond the sphere of my periphery, but it wasn't enough to illuminate anything.

"Why can't I see anything?" I asked Hilary in frustration.

"Because I don't want you to. Since you decided to nose around Arty's business, I decided you should join him," she said, and I felt the boat turn to the right slightly.

"Join him? Do you mean he's still alive?"

"Oh, yes. On the small island near Blue Ridge Cove. The island that nobody visits because it's covered in poison ivy and goose droppings."

"How has he survived all this time? It's been four months since he disappeared!" I shifted myself again, still trying to find the edge of the net.

"I told you not to bother," she said. "I made sure he has everything he needs; Arty believes he is living in paradise. He wants for nothing except maybe sunscreen; there's not much shelter there." Her voice gave me the impression that she was just casually waving off this concern, as if it was nothing to worry about.

"He has been on an island that is covered in poison ivy and goose poop for four months, and you are telling me that he thinks it is paradise? How is that possible? Babs said you weren't that good at illusions," I jeered. Maybe I could provoke her into talking more.

"Ha! I'm very good at illusions, but I didn't need to use them for Arty; he was easy. A lonely guy, depressed because of his breakup with his wife—it didn't take much to get him out to the island. My Siren song works best on the lonely hearts of men, and its effects last much longer than my illusions," Hilary boasted with conviction.

"Well, it must have taken more skill than you expected, because it took you six months to make it happen. Whatever you did, you were slowly driving Arty insane between November of last year until his disappearance this past May," I said, trying to poke the bear some more. I could sense her getting angrier; the angrier she got, the more I could see. It seemed that when she lost control of her emotions, she also lost some control over her illusions.

"That wasn't my fault," she growled.

"Oh really? Then just whose fault was it? Or was it just your incompetence? You were obviously trading in secrets—ineptly, if I do say so myself—and Arty caught you. He threatened to report you, and in turn, you used your so-called 'powers' to try and stop him," I said, making air quotes with my one free hand.

"Incompetence! It's not my fault that I am a genetic mess and that my powers only work sometimes!" she snapped. My vision cleared even more; I could make out the lines of the net against my face in the slight glow of the rising moon. I could tell there was no other light source on the boat; Hilary was navigating in the dark, trying to avoid the notice of the residents around the lake.

"What's that supposed to mean, 'a genetic mess'?"

"Exactly what it sounds like. Most of my line is plain old human, no specialties, but my great grandmother was a Siren, and my father's family come from a line of Huli Jing."

"I know what a Siren is," I said, suddenly connecting the Greek myth with the triptych in Odeon's office. "But what exactly is a Huli Jing?" I asked, playing dumb.

"Chinese fox shifters, illusionists, but the power only presents in the females, and there hasn't been a daughter in my father's line in nearly eighty years, at least not one who lived," she explained.

"So, what, you used Huli Jing illusions to drive Arty mad?" I waited. I could hear her grumbling under her breath; she was getting angrier by the moment. The more upset she got, the more I could see my surroundings.

I could now tell that my first impressions were correct, and I took in the situation trying to figure out a way to escape. I was trapped under some sort of weighted fishing net that appeared to have been latched to the boat at various points with D-rings. I wriggled around some more, hoping to reach some of the D-rings now that I could at least kind of see where they were.

"No, that was the Siren bloodline; I used Siren Song. As a Siren I didn't even need to try; I could bewitch him with just the inflection of my voice. It worked perfectly to discredit him, and to make him appear insane in case he had reported my actions to the chief. I needed people to think that he might have committed suicide or disappeared of his own volition," Hilary explained.

"So let me get this straight . . . you were selling information online about the special people of Blackwater Lake. Arty caught you, so you slowly drove him insane with your Siren Song, and then you lured him out to some island of rock?" I let it sink in. "The one thing I don't get is the birds. What the heck was up with all the references to birds?"

Hilary didn't get a chance to answer, because at that moment I heard the crunch of the boat's aluminum hull against a gravel beach. Hilary killed the motor, stood up, and stepped over me to jump off the bow, landing hard in the gravel. She grabbed the tow line and, with effort, dragged the boat up onto the shore. I could now see perfectly; the strain of hauling the boat up seemed to have sapped the last of her energy. I was able to wrench my arm out from underneath me and twist myself around a little more. I edged quietly and slowly toward the D-ring on my right, squeezing my fingers through the netting; I tried to unclip it.

"I said not to do that!" Hilary shouted, and whacked my fingers with a piece of driftwood she had picked up off the beach. She stood over me as I lay on the bottom of the boat; her right foot was propped up on the rim of the hull, and her black and pink wellington boot dripped water onto me. I cradled my fingers against my chest; at least one of them felt broken.

"What's your next move, Hilary? You've got me out to the island, but now you've got to leave me here. I'm not susceptible to your Siren Song, and your illusionary abilities seem spent," I taunted.

"You're an idiot," she spat at me.

"Really, how so? The way I see it, the second you try to unhook this net, I will overpower you and break free."

"It's not me that you'll have to contend with," she said, taking a step away from the boat.

I strained to peer up and around the edge of the hull; I just couldn't get a good angle to see anything. I needn't have tried. Moments after Hilary stepped back, a masculine face leaned over the boat and stared at me. I didn't recognize him. His beard was long and shaggy, his skin was sunburned, and his hair hung over his eyes. I didn't need to recognize him, though; there was only one person this could be . . . Arthur Odeon.

"Arty, dear," Hilary said with a slight song in her voice. "Take her out of the boat and bring her up on shore," she commanded.

Odeon reached into the boat, and that's when I realized he had a knife in his hand. He cut through the netting, not even bothering to unclip the rings, and gathered the netting down and around me. I was bound just as tight as before, and he dragged me like a netted fish up and over the edge of the boat hull. Every part of my body banged against the hull. I took an especially sharp blow against my midsection and screamed in pain. I landed hard on the gravel beach. I could already feel the bruises forming on my hip and thigh, and I doubled over from the pain in my side. I would be one hurting puppy tomorrow if I ever got out of this situation.

"Arty, this is your new companion. She's going to keep you company since I can't always be here," Hilary sang.

"But it's you I love; I don't want to be with anyone else," Arty said, his voice low and raspy, like he was dehydrated.

"I know, my sweetheart, but I have many responsibilities and cannot stay here. You will be well taken care of, as always." She reached up her hand as if she was going to caress his face, but she stopped short of touching him.

I couldn't blame her, really. Arty was a filthy, tangled mess of hair. His beard was entwined with various twigs and dirt, and there was a poison ivy rash on his cheekbone. I couldn't fathom what he had been eating and drinking all this time out here. In the moonlight, I could see that the island was little more than a pile of rocks with brush and dead trees surrounding it.

"I need you," Arty pleaded. "I can't live without you; every time you leave, I feel like I will die. . . ."

"Arty," I called from my uncomfortable place on the ground, as I gritted my teeth in pain. He glanced down at me but didn't really seem to see me. "You need to let me go, Arty. I can help you keep her here. Don't you want her to stay here forever?" I said soothingly, playing into his delusion.

"Forever?" he rasped.

"Yes, I can help you keep her here, with you. Forever."

"Shut up!" Hilary yelled at me. Then, turning to Arty, she cooed, "Arty, you don't need her to get in between the two of us. She's just here to be your servant, to wait on you and ensure you have everything you need."

"You don't need a servant. You need Hilary. Hilary is the only thing that will keep you from dying," I said reassuringly.

"I need you, Hilary!" Arthur cried.

Letting go of the netting, and me with it, he lunged toward Hilary and tried to wrap his arms around her. Realizing my opportunity, I struggled out of the net. As I stood up, I doubled over in pain from my abdomen and had to bite my lower lip to keep from crying out. I forced myself to stand up as fast as my bare feet would allow. I wasn't going to be able to run very far, having kicked off my shoes before falling asleep on the couch earlier.

Hilary dodged Odeon's embrace. She was dressed in proper footwear and was much better fed and hydrated than Arty; she also had the advantage of being slight and fast on her feet.

"Arty, my love, you don't need to force me to stay. I told you I will always be yours, but we have a servant who can help us when we are here. You just need to help me catch her again and take her back to the palace," Hilary said, using her most persuasive sing-song voice.

"Oh, please! Look around you, Arthur; there's no palace here. There's barely any 'here' here," I scoffed. Somehow, I had to break him out of his reverie.

"You have no idea what you are talking about. Hilary, my love, has given me everything I need to be happy," Odeon growled.

"Everything but herself," I said, and pointed at Hilary.

"Everything but herself," Odeon repeated mindlessly.

"Arty, you can't listen to her. She's trying to poison you against me; she's a serpent," Hilary's melodic voice sang.

"I need you, Hilary; she can't poison me against you. She's right, you must stay here with me!" Arthur cried.

As Hilary took an involuntary step back, away from Odeon, her boot caught on a rock and her ankle twisted. She went down with a yelp and landed on her backside. Arthur charged toward her, distressed that she had fallen. But his abrupt move to help her up only made her more anxious.

With both of them distracted, I picked my way over the rocks and gravel back to the boat. I was leaning over to push it back into the lake when I felt a hand grasp my disheveled hair and yank me backward. Once again, I fell hard onto my bruised buttocks and sat looking up into Hilary's face.

"Nice try," she said. "But Arty would never hurt me. He loves me, the stupid fool," she added, muttering under her breath.

"You can't keep this up," I said, trying to appeal to her rational side now, whatever was left of it. "The illusion, the Siren Song, they are taxing your energy. Just how much longer do you think you can sustain this?" I asked.

"I don't need to; once I leave here, I'm done with you both," she snapped. "I'm leaving Blackwater Lake. There's no way I will stick around here with two general managers disappearing."

"Well, that makes sense," I said, resorting to my original tactic of egging her on since it seemed to have worked so well the first time. "Why didn't you just kill Arthur in the first place and be done with it?"

"I'm not a killer," she said haughtily, tossing her hair back.

"Not a killer? But if you leave us here now, we are surely both going to die. How will we survive if you don't bring us food and water?" I asked, assuming that was what she had been doing for Arthur all these months.

"Bringing food and water," she said disdainfully. "No. I haven't been doing any such thing. Arty, sweetums, what's for dinner tonight?" she called over to Odeon. He was now seated on a rock, watching our exchange with vacant eyes.

"Fish and goose goes well with some of those plants over there," he said, pointing toward a tall stand of weeds in the shallow water around the island's edge. Even in the moonlight, I could see the tell-tale shape of cattails. "Oh, and the lake water is pristine; I can serve it up in my best crystal for you, my love," Arthur said in response to Hilary's question.

I felt bile churn in my stomach. Odeon must have been just getting by on whatever he could find to eat on this pile of rocks. I doubted he even had a fire to cook with since someone on the mainland would have been likely to see the smoke. Hilary Wen may not have been a killer by the standard definition of the word, but she certainly wasn't a sane person. And now that Odeon had been subjected to her illusions and Siren Song, he wasn't anywhere near sane, either.

"Oh, Arty, that sounds delicious," I said, with as much sincerity as I could muster. "You should convince Hilary to stay and enjoy it. I'm sure she wants to eat dinner with us—you know, like a date?"

Odeon jumped to his feet and charged toward Hilary once more, grabbing her excitedly by placing an arm around her waist and drawing her close. She leaned back as far as she could, trying to keep her face away from his disgusting beard and rancid breath.

"Stay," Odeon rasped with longing in his voice.

Taking advantage of the distraction, I again attempted to go for the boat. This time, I pushed it back into the water before a hand firmly grabbed my elbow and yanked me back. I didn't have to look to see who it was; the hand was rough and calloused. I spun around and found myself face-to-face with Arthur again. His vile breath churned my stomach, and it was all I could do to keep from vomiting. Hilary had her arm looped through his unoccupied hand and was coaxing him into restraining me.

"Of course I'll stay, Arty. I just need you to secure her and then bring me the boat," she cooed.

"The boat?" he asked, perplexed. "But you'll leave if you have the boat." It seemed that her Siren Song wasn't enough to overcome *all* of his rational thought.

"No, I told you I would stay, and I will," Hilary placated.

"Okay, if you promise," he growled.

Odeon yanked me back toward the net on the rocks. I tried to resist, to escape his grasp, but his hand was like a vice on my arm. He forced me down onto my knees, yanked my hands behind my back, and wrapped the remains of the net around my wrists; but as he pulled the knot tight, I held my wrists slightly apart at the last moment. As a result, the net was tied more loosely around my wrists than Odeon had intended. He pushed me down even farther and kicked me in the midsection. I once again fell onto my right side and hip, adding to the mosaic of bruises that were forming on my body.

Arty then turned around robotically and waded waist-deep into the water, over to where the boat gently bumped against the rocks with the rhythm of the waves. Then, I realized that the waves had picked up their pace, but there was no wind to cause them to do so. And in a lake, the waves only strengthened when there was wind, a storm, or a boat passing by.

A boat! I thought and wriggled my wrists out of the netting. I painfully sat upright and looked out at the lake. Sure enough, there were three boats with bright spotlights bearing down on the island. They also had red and blue lightbars flashing on top of their activity towers.

The boats pulled up to the rocky island, and people jumped into the shallow water with their guns drawn and aimed their guns at Hilary as they moved toward the beach; they walked past Arthur but didn't pay him much heed.

"Hilary Wen, put your hands up and get down on the ground," Chief Baxter yelled from where he stood in ankle-deep water. Just then, Odeon rushed behind him and tried to bowl him over, but the officer behind the chief to his left intercepted Odeon and knocked him into the water with a splash; Arty sat there staring stupidly up at the officer.

"That's my Hilary . . ." he rasped. "She's mine."

"Stay down!" the officer said, and pointed his gun at Odeon. I could see Detective Daniels' name badge glinting in the spotlight.

"Hilary, this is my last warning. Get down on the ground, face down!" the chief cried, turning his attention back to Hilary. She complied, and the third officer, a woman, rushed in to handcuff Hilary as fast as the water and rocks would allow. The chief lowered his gun and trudged forward, reaching down to help me up.

"Are you alright?" he asked me.

"Bruised and battered, but other than that, fine, I think," I said through gritted teeth, wincing at the pain. "How did you know where to find me?" I asked, shocked to find him all the way out on the south side of the lake.

"Jet," he said, frankly. I heard Jet bark in acknowledgment from the closest boat.

"What? How is that possible? When I last saw him, he was locked in my house . . . I think, or maybe on my dock. I'm not really sure; it's all very confusing because of Hilary's illusions," I said wearily. The adrenaline was starting to wear off.

"Let's get you back to shore; we can discuss all this later." He helped me onto the boat. I groaned in pain as I lowered myself onto one of the seats. The chief wrapped a wool blanket around me, and I felt a flutter in my stomach that had nothing to do with my injuries. A blush came over my face as he knelt beside me and secured the blanket.

"You really had us all worried," he said, and began to look me over from head to toe. My feet were cut up, and I was covered with bruises, but he decided that I was well enough to make it to shore without any immediate medical attention. He stood back up and went to supervise the rest of his officers as they loaded a handcuffed Hilary and a weak and bewildered Arthur onto the other two boats.

I groaned and leaned back in my seat, pulling the wool blanket tighter. Jet came over to my side and laid his head in my lap.

"You're a really good boy, buddy," I said, slipping my left hand out from under the blanket to scritch him behind the ears. I closed my eyes and found myself drifting off to sleep. Less than half an hour later, I was shaken awake by a hand on my shoulder.

"Ma'am, why don't you come with me? We'll get you checked out." It was a paramedic. Jet was still at my side; his tail was wagging, and he seemed happy to have arrived back at the main dock near the clubhouse.

I let the paramedic gently guide me off the boat and up the path to a waiting ambulance. The pathway's cool, smooth slate paving felt soothing on my cut feet. By the time I reached the ambulance, though, my body had started to shiver despite the warm night air.

"She's going into shock." The first paramedic coaxed me onto the gurney and hooked me up to monitors. He shined his penlight into my eyes.

"Is she bleeding?" the second paramedic asked.

"Only minor cuts on her feet and hands, that I can see. Her finger is at an odd angle, might be broken," the first paramedic said. My breathing became labored, and my pulse began to slow on the monitor screen. I heard Jet whine plaintively in the distance and wanted to comfort him, but my arms felt heavy, and my eyelids started to drop. I lost consciousness.

* * *

I woke up in what appeared to be a hospital. I managed to sit up slightly, but my head throbbed, and I was constrained by the IV that was hooked up to my arm. Thirsty and sore, I looked around the room, trying to get my bearings. A young boy, about twelve years old, was curled up asleep in an armchair in the corner of the room. He was pale with wavy, dark brown hair, slightly tousled and long enough to flop down over his eyes, and had a slender build and prominent cheekbones. He reminded me of a very young Timothy Chalamet.

I was utterly confused. The last thing that I remembered was being in the ambulance. I must have blacked out before they took me to the hospital. That made sense, but who was the boy in the chair?

The door to the room opened, and Babs breezed in carrying a coffee.

"Oh, you're awake," she said, not unkindly.

"Yeah, and I'm dying of thirst. Is there any water?" I asked. She grabbed a pitcher from the tray at the foot of the bed and poured me a cup of ice water. I drank it greedily and thrust my hand out for another cup; this one, I sipped more slowly.

"What happened?" I asked. "And who is he?" I gestured to the sleeping boy.

"You had internal bleeding from blunt force trauma to your abdomen, and you started to go into shock," Babs said. "The ambulance brought you here to the town's clinic, which also serves as our hospital. The doctors managed to stop the bleeding without surgery. You also have a broken finger and a fractured rib," she explained.

"And who is the kid?" I asked again.

"That is . . . Jet," Babs responded.

EPILOGUE

I was released from the hospital on Friday, the morning after the Hilary incident, with some medication for pain and instructions to rest and stay hydrated. Clive had called me when I got home and told me not to worry about coming to work until at least Wednesday. He apologized for the whole situation and lamented that my first week had been "so rough."

Understatement of the year, I thought.

"I'm not sure how you got roped into the middle of all this, darlin', but it sure wasn't fair to you," he apologized.

"Thanks, Clive; it's partly my own doing, sticking my nose into business where it doesn't belong," I admitted.

"All the same, it should never have happened, and I'm sorry that it did," he said, his warm Georgia drawl putting me at ease and reassuring me of his sincerity.

"I can't argue with that," I said.

Although he knew I was aware of his special ability, we avoided discussing it on the phone. Neither of us wanted to talk about the elephant—or rather the dragon—in the room. Clive wished me a quick recovery, and we clicked off the line.

Shortly after the call ended, there was a knock at my door. I started to get up and answer it, but the door opened before I could.

"Don't get up," Chief Baxter said, striding down the hallway toward the living room, where I sat on the couch sipping sparkling water.

"Sure, just let yourself in," I said sarcastically. "I'm pretty sure I locked that front door."

"You did, but Babs gave me the spare key last night. She wanted to make sure that I checked in on you," he answered, apparently oblivious to my sarcasm.

"How reassuring," I said sarcastically, annoyed that Babs was meddling.

"Are you mad at me? I saved your life last night," he said, without a breath of modesty.

"I'm a little mad at everyone right now," I answered. "This whole situation could have been avoided if you people had been honest with me from the get-go."

"Honest with you? About what exactly?"

"Odeon's disappearance, the nature and purpose of this community . . . everything!" I shouted, taking out twenty-four hours' worth of anger, frustration, and pent-up emotions on the town's chief of police.

"Would you have believed us if we told you everything?" he asked calmly.

"Probably not," I replied sheepishly.

"There's a reason why we do things the way we do. Ninety days gives normal outsiders enough time to experience something out of the ordinary, something that they just can't explain. Then, when we break the news to them, it's not as unbelievable as it otherwise would have been. Frankly, you're absorbing this information much better than anyone could have imagined. It's almost as if you are already part of the community," he said, taking a seat on the ottoman across from me.

"In my case, I think you should have made an exception," I grumbled.

"How were we supposed to know that you were going to go and start your own investigation?" he argued.

"Well, it's not like you were doing anything," I snapped.

"Detective Daniels and I had been investigating Arthur's disappearance for months. The evidence we had pointed toward Hilary, but we didn't have enough to act upon. We needed enough to get a warrant for her arrest; up until last night, everything we had was circumstantial."

"How could you have missed a man living marooned on a rock on the south side of the lake?" I asked incredulously.

"Hilary put up an illusion around the rock. Not much of one, but enough so that when we looked at it, we only saw what we expected to see: a barren rock covered in poison ivy and geese," he explained.

"She wasn't that powerful. How could she have done all of this on her own? She said that her powers didn't always work as she wanted them to because of her mixed upbringing."

"She may have had help. We believe that one of the buyers she was working with may have sent her something that helped her amplify her powers. We found an amulet on her when we processed her at the police station."

"So . . . let me get this straight. Hilary Wen was selling information about Blackwater Lake's special people on the internet. What was her motive to do so in the first place?"

"According to some emails that we found on her computer, she never really felt like she belonged in this community. She had apparently always felt like a misfit," the chief explained.

"A misfit? But she was in several positions of power, both as the secretary of the board and the secretary of the Ladies Auxiliary." I was confused.

"Still, because she wasn't *that* powerful, at least not magically, it appears that she felt like she was marginalized by the rest of the magical community," he explained.

"So, she sold the town's secrets on the internet? Why? Money? Status?" I scoffed.

"It appears that she had made some seriously shifty friends, and they preyed upon her feelings of inadequacy. They talked her into selling Blackwater Lake's secrets for money and perceived power over the people that she felt were alienating her. But whoever they were, they covered their tracks well; we only found Hilary's side of the email conversations. We were lucky to find the information that we did. Those friends, whoever they were, seem to have disappeared, but not before they tried to help her to eliminate a threat to their operation. That threat being Arthur Odeon."

"I'm still not entirely sure how Hilary thought that marooning him on an island was a good idea; and why did it take her so long to lure him out there?"

"She needed to eliminate him. At the same time, she wanted to discredit him so that if he reported her, people would think he was crazy. So, she lured him out onto the water on the night of the Halloween storm. That was when this all began. She needed to lure him out to the lake because her Siren Song works best when she is surrounded by water."

"But on Halloween night he came back with a bundle in his hands," I said. "If I recall the story correctly, he had implied that the bundle was some type of bird that he had to save." I was trying to get more information out of this conversation than the chief appeared to be willing to divulge given his stone-faced cop expression.

"Arty told me that he thought he had rescued some sort of bird. Thinking back on it now, I actually think he may have said that it was an osprey that he rescued."

"Was there an osprey in Odeon's arms?" I said, poking the conversation along.

"No, just a bundle of rags."

"This is all so insane; it's hard to wrap my head around; and what is up with all the weird references to birds? At first, I thought they were clues leading to his ex-wife, but I was obviously wrong."

"The birds were related to Hilary's Siren Song. A true Siren can transform into a bird-woman. Hilary, being only part Siren and part Huli Jing, generated illusions of birds instead. Apparently, birds were the easiest thing for her to project," the chief explained.

"Thank you for making my point for me; you knew who she was and what her abilities were! How could she have possibly harassed him for six months without anyone noticing? I mean, Odeon all but told you that a Siren was the cause of the problem; he redecorated his entire office as a tribute," I argued.

"It wasn't proof. Besides, no one knew about Wen's Siren background until after the fact. It's not like we have a database of everyone's abilities, this isn't the X-files! Half of the people here are non-paranormal folks. They're just people who have had some experience with paranormal phenomena or who are incredibly gifted in a non-paranormal way. To be honest, most of us thought that Hilary was living here just because she had become privy to some paranormal information in her past career; no one thought that she was as powerful as she turned out to be," the chief said defensively.

"You could have looked at his computer files and emails like I did. He was a missing person; I'm sure you could have gotten a warrant or permission from Clive to do so! I found everything within three days!" I protested.

"We did look, but we didn't find anything. We think that Hilary somehow managed to get us some dummy files. We're just not sure how she did it, seeing as the files came to us via Ned," he explained.

"But Ned had Odeon's original files; that's how I got the information," I argued.

"Exactly," the chief said bluntly.

"Maybe one of her contacts has a hack into the computer system, which would explain how she knew that I was investigating," I mused.

"Ned is looking into it."

I sighed, exasperated, and leaned back on the couch. I took a long sip of my sparkling water, which went down the wrong pipe and made me cough and sputter. The coughing jarred my bruised body, and I groaned, wrapping my arms around my waist. The chief jumped to his feet, looking worried and unsure of what to do. I raised my hand as the coughing subsided, signaling that the chief could stand down.

"I'm fine," I rasped, "wrong pipe, that's all."

"Can I get you anything?" The chief was solicitous, as always.

"No, really, I'm fine. Thanks," I said, sounding more like myself. Just then, there was a timid knock at the door. I groaned again and made to get up off the couch.

"I'll get it," the chief said with more eagerness than was needed. He walked down the hallway, and I heard the door open. I tried to crane my neck around to see what was going on, but it hurt too much, so I decided to wait and see what would happen next.

Very little can surprise me now, I thought. But I was wrong.

The chief walked back down the hallway with Jet, in human form, trailing shyly behind him. I hadn't expected to see the kid again. After my conversation with Babs in the hospital, she'd woke him up and took him home. She didn't even explain how this boy could be the same Jet that I had known for the past week as a springer spaniel.

"C'mon in, buddy," the chief said gently. He gestured for Jet to sit in one of the chairs; he took the other.

"Hi, Jet," I said with hesitation. I had never spoken to him before, at least not when he was in human form.

"Hi, Miss Kat," he said politely.

"I owe you my gratitude for saving me last night," I said with sincerity. "I'm not really sure how you did it, but the chief says that he was able to find me because of you. Thank you."

"You're welcome," he said automatically, looking a little embarrassed to be thanked by an adult.

"It seems Hilary lured you out of the house with an illusion of Jet going down to the dock," said the chief. "When you ran outside, the real Jet tried to follow you, but you had closed the screen door behind you. He couldn't return to his human form fast enough to open it and catch up with you before Hilary pulled you into the boat. So instead, he decided to call for help using your cellphone, which you had left on your counter."

"Rewind," I said, "this is all a bit much for me to follow. You're a dog?" I asked Jet.

"Shifter, human to dog," he said quietly.

"How come you never introduced yourself to me as a human?" I asked.

"I wasn't allowed to," he answered, embarrassed.

"Right. The secrets in this special place just keep piling up," I growled, and Jet stood up and dashed out the sliding glass door, heading down to the dock.

"Don't blame him," the chief said.

"I don't! The poor kid was just doing what he was told. I blame all the adults who should have known better."

"He probably wouldn't have shown you his human form anyway. He's had a tough year; he's rather shy around new people unless he's in dog form," the chief explained.

"What's his story, anyway?" I asked, hoping that I would finally get a straight answer.

"Like he said, he's a dog shifter."

"That's not what I meant, and you know it. Where does he live? Who are his parents? How can he spend nearly a full week at my house, and nobody even wondered where he was?" I clarified.

"He's a ward of the town. He lives by the school in an old house originally built for the groundskeeper about fifty years ago. Bella Knox, the town's social worker, keeps an eye on him, as does the middle school's principal. Frankly, all of us keep a watchful eye on the poor kid."

"He's an orphan? What happened?" I asked.

"He used to live just outside of the HOA with his parents. It wasn't a glamorous life, but he wasn't neglected or abused. Not all of the special people in this town can afford to live in the subdivision; many others live within the town but on the outskirts of the HOA." The chief continued: "Anyway, his parents died last year; they both succumbed to an opioid overdose. They had gotten a bad batch of drugs that were unfortunately laced with fentanyl."

"Oh, good Lord, that poor boy," I said, tears stinging my eyes. "How can such a thing happen here, in this place full of special people?" I asked, confused.

"We're all human, even if we're special. We fall prey to the same vices and problems that the rest of the world faces. Why do you think I have a job here?" the chief asked, rhetorically.

"I need to apologize to him. He must think that I was mad at him," I said with concern, and I tried, again, to stand up. The chief stood and reached out a hand to help pull me up to my feet.

"Thanks," I said, feeling flushed at his touch. I had to remind myself that he was engaged to Jessica.

"C'mon, I'll help you down to the dock, and we can finish telling you what happened last night. You need to stretch your muscles a little bit anyway."

I slipped my feet into moccasins, and the chief offered me his elbow. I linked my arm to his, and we slowly descended to the dock. Jet was sitting at the edge, still in human form, holding a handful of rocks that he was skipping out into the water one by one.

"Jet," I said hesitantly, as the chief helped me sit in an Adirondack chair. He remained standing with arms crossed, looking down at the boy in concern. Jet didn't turn around to look at me, but I continued anyway, trying to reassure him. "I'm sorry I sounded so angry, but please know that I wasn't angry at you. I am so grateful for everything you did to help me last night." He continued to skip rocks and refused to look up at me.

"He really was a hero last night," the chief said. "I had already been warned that something might happen. Jessica listened to your conversations with Wen at the luncheon, and she knew something wasn't right. She was aware of my investigation into Hilary, so she grew concerned when the two of you started talking so cryptically at the table."

"Jessica was concerned about me?" I asked skeptically. That garnered a little chuckle and a snort out of Jet, which reassured me that he was listening. Perhaps his mood was coming around.

"Yes, she's not a bad person," the chief said defensively. "When she realized that Jet was going to come home with you last night in his dog form, she felt a little bit better about the situation, but she still gave me a heads up."

"Well, that explains why she was pacing around in the lobby of the clubhouse. But I find it hard to believe that everyone was banking on Jet to be the hero; he's just a kid! No offense, Jet."

He just shrugged in response.

"No one was expecting Jet to do anything, but they knew that if he was with you, he would smell, see, and hear danger long before you did. He could alert you to a problem like any dog would."

I huffed at this pronouncement.

"Shifter dog or not, he's still just a kid; you could have at least set a watch on my house," I protested.

"We did; that's how we got to you so fast. We had a watch both on land and on the water. When we got the call, we deployed right away. We had to come past this dock, and when we did, Jet was sitting exactly where he is now, except in dog form. He jumped in the water and swam toward my boat; I had to double back and pull him up out of the water. I was worried that he was going to drown," the chief said. He paused to look with concern and compassion at the boy.

"He shifted back to human and used his heightened senses to help us find which direction Hilary had taken you. Even with his help, it was harder to find you than we had expected. Hilary's illusions were still in effect. But ultimately, we did find you and, well . . . you were there for the rest of it."

"What happened to Hilary and to Arty?" I asked.

"Hilary was sent to jail and is awaiting a hearing. She doesn't seem to have the good sense to keep her mouth shut—she has been blabbering about how important she is and how she had every right to do what she did to Arty. She keeps saying that we will 'rue the day' when her secret allies find out that she's in jail. She has pretty much confessed to everything."

"Secret allies?" I asked. "Are these the same people who gave her the amulet and who may have helped her hack into the HOA computer system?"

"We think so, but whoever they are, I doubt that anyone is coming for her. I'm sure they see her as expendable."

"What about Arty?" I asked again.

"Arty is going to need a lot of care. We transported him to a special hospital for paranormals in Richmond. He's suffering from sun exposure, E.coli bacteria, dehydration, malnutrition—and, of course, he's been psychologically tormented by Hilary and her illusions."

"There's a special hospital for paranormals?" I asked, somehow shocked once again.

"Yes, it operates under the cover of a research institute for people with rare diseases," he explained.

"So, Arty is a paranormal? I never did get the chance to ask Babs," I said.

"Yes, cat shifter."

"Cat shifter? And he was married to Robin, who had all of those birds for pets?" I asked, beginning to understand why their marriage hadn't been successful.

"Yeah, I never really understood why that marriage got off the ground in the first place. To top it all off, Robin is a swan shifter."

"Wow, it's no wonder they were so at odds with each other. Sounds like they were incompatible from the beginning, but maybe it was an 'opposites attract' kind of situation."

I paused briefly, taking all this information in and thinking about how I had been certain that Robin had been the bad guy just because of her birds. If Sirens were bird women, as legend had it, then it made sense that bird illusions would be the easiest for Hilary to create. I should have realized that Robin was far too obvious a scapegoat for the disappearance of her ex-husband.

Still processing all this new information, I took a deep breath and soaked up some of the sun. It wasn't nearly as hot as it had been the past few days, and sitting here and listening to the water was relaxing. The three of us fell into an amicable silence for a few moments. It was Jet who spoke first.

"Miss Kat?" he queried.

"Yeah, bud?" I prompted.

"Can I stay with you, at least for a little while? I can be a helper while you are getting better," he asked hopefully.

"I don't know, Jet," I said hesitantly, looking toward the chief for guidance.

"It's up to you. We can arrange for him to stay here if you want," the chief said.

"I . . . I don't know if that would be appropriate. I only have the one other room, and frankly, that room is just a bit creepy with the half-painted mural," I hedged.

"Willow can repaint it. And having Jet stay here would be better than him staying by himself in an old cabin," the chief added quietly, though I knew Jet had heard him anyway.

"Don't repaint it!" Jet cried. "I like it; in fact, I wish it was back the way it used to be."

"'Used to be'? Did you ever see it before it was painted over?" I asked him, groaning as I sat up a little straighter.

"Yes, it used to belong to my friend Jacob, before he died. We used to play together all the time when I was in elementary school."

My heart broke for this child; it sounded like he could use some security and consistency in his life.

"Okay," I said, and Jet perked up for the first time that morning. "You can stay here, and I'll see if Willow knows of anyone who can restore the mural. But there's no more skipping school and running around town, even in dog form," I scolded.

"Okay!" Jet agreed; he seemed happy to agree to anything now that he knew I was going to take him in.

"Can I still go to the concert tonight?" he asked.

"Sure, we'll both go," I said.

"Are you sure you're up for that?" I heard the concern in the chief's voice.

"I'll ask Andy to save me a seat on the deck so I can duck out when I want. Jet, you can hang out with your friends near the beach, but I expect you to come right home after the concert at nine."

"Yes, ma'am," he answered with respect.

"Well, then let me help you back up to the house, and I'll leave you two to get to know each other better. Jet, I'll inform Ms. Knox about your new arrangement and ask her to bring your belongings over here."

Chief Baxter helped me back up the hill to the house and onto a chair at the kitchen island. Without being asked, Jet immediately started buzzing around the kitchen, looking for things to make for lunch. The chief ensured that Jet and I had everything we needed and then headed out the front door. He was not on duty that night but would be at the concert with Jessica. He said that he hoped to see me there. My heart deflated again at the reminder of his fiancé.

Jet and I hung around for the rest of the afternoon. At one point, I napped upstairs while he watched something on the TV. My phone buzzed, waking me up, and I groggily reached for it on my nightstand.

"Hello," I said, instinctively knowing who it was without having to look at the caller ID.

"Oh, thank God you're alive!" Penny screamed in my ear.

"Nice to talk to you too, Penny, but what do you mean by alive?" I asked.

"Apparently, you listed me as your emergency contact. I got a call last night from that chief of police of yours telling me that you were in the hospital."

"He's not 'my' chief of police," I argued.

"Are you sure? He sounded super-hot on the phone," she teased.

"Quite sure. What did he tell you?" I asked, unsure how much he had said about the paranormal parts of the situation.

"He just said that you had an encounter with Odeon's kidnapper, that you had been injured and suffered some internal bleeding, but that you were safe in the hospital and recovering," she said.

"That's it?" I asked.

"Yes. I offered to come down to the hospital, but he told me not to bother since you were sleeping, and he promised that you would call me in the morning. Which you didn't!" she complained.

"He must have forgotten to tell me he called you. I had no idea that he had done so," I said.

"Well, he was very cryptic. You *have* to tell me everything!" she exclaimed.

"Everything?" I was unsure of how much I should say.

"Ev-e-ry-thing," Penny said, emphasizing each syllable.

I wanted to tell her about the paranormal parts of the tale, but I was pretty sure that she would assume I had hit my head and would try to send me back to the hospital. So, I told her as much of the story as I dared: that Hilary had shown up at my house while I was sleeping, dragged me off to the rocky island where Odeon was being kept, and attempted to maroon me there as well. I explained that Jessica had warned the chief about a possible threat, so he had set up surveillance and was therefore able to rescue me quickly. I left out the parts about Hilary's illusions. And, regretfully, I left out the parts about Jet's heroic efforts.

"So, Hilary Wen had been selling secrets on the internet, and she somehow tricked Arthur Odeon out to a goose-crap-covered rock in the middle of nowhere? How is that possible?" Penny asked after she had recovered from the shock of the story.

"She used hallucinogens," I explained; it was the closest answer to the truth that I could give her.

"Wow! And the dragon, was that part of her misinformation campaign, her plan to make Odeon look insane?" she asked.

"Something like that," I said.

"Well, I'm just glad that you are okay. Who told you to start an investigation and to stick your nose where it doesn't belong?" she asked sincerely.

"You did," I answered, and we both burst out laughing. I laughed until I doubled up in pain and my sides hurt. We hung up and I took some pain medication, then drifted back to sleep.

* * *

At around six o'clock, Jet and I went to the clubhouse for dinner. We had called ahead, and Jet took his burger to go and hurried down to the waterfront. Andy set me up with a comfortable deck chair overlooking the lake. A server brought a glass of red wine and a plate of nachos to snack on.

"Is there anything else that I can get for you?" Andy asked nervously. I got the impression that he was walking on eggshells, not sure how to treat his brand-new boss who had just been hired, then abducted, beaten, battered, and bruised, all within the past week.

"Andy, relax. I'm fine, there's no need to worry. If I need something, I'll flag down one of the servers, just like anyone else."

He let out a breath that he had been holding and visibly relaxed.

"If you need anything, anything at all, just ask," he said, and plastered on his most professional smile before hurrying off to take care of some other patrons and event necessities.

I looked down at the beach and saw Jet. He was in human form, walking around with a small group of boys and girls his age. They were laughing and joking, and he looked happy.

I felt a shadow move over me, blocking the setting sun, and looked up to see Babs with a cocktail in hand. She was dressed in a denim skirt and a novelty T-shirt that featured the Nirvana face logo, over which she wore an oversized flannel shirt with the sleeves rolled up. On her feet, she had a pair of black combat boots.

"Hi, Babs. I see that you dressed for the occasion." I smiled at her.

"Glad to see you up and about."

She sat across from me. Just then the band kicked off their first set with a cover of the Bare-Naked Ladies song "One Week."

"You've had a heck of a first week," she said, "no pun intended." She looked out at the band on the barge in the water. Her timing was perfect.

"Ain't that the truth," I said, sipping my wine.

"I hear that Jet is moving in with you. So, I guess that means that you are sticking around for a while." Her tone didn't indicate whether or not she was happy about that turn of events.

"Yes, I am. You can't get rid of me that easily," I said, winking at her.

"Good, we need someone who can handle the chaos of this place, and you have a good head on your shoulders. You never know what's going to happen next around here." She said this with a smile and gave my knee a firm pat. I winced; she had managed to find one of my yellowing bruises.

"Sorry." She smiled apologetically.

"Well, I just hope I can live up to your expectations," I said. "Here's to chaos." I raised my glass for a toast.

"To chaos!" we said in unison. We clinked glasses, sat back, and enjoyed the concert as the sun set over Blackwater Lake.

STAY TUNED FOR MORE CHAOS

* * *

ABOUT THE AUTHOR

Carolyn Brodeur is originally from Massachusetts and moved to Virginia in 2005. She is married to a wonderful husband and has one son. In college, she studied English and writing. Her dream was to one day become a fiction author. She enjoyed reading sci-fi, paranormal, and mystery book series growing up, but she never found her preferred genre to write until she discovered cozy mysteries and started working for a homeowners association.

The unique dynamic of a small HOA community that exists in its own micro-verse became the perfect setting for Carolyn's cozy mystery book. Her works are entirely fictional, but working for an HOA has given Carolyn plenty of inspiration. At times, real life even outpaces her stories; she can frequently be heard saying "I can't make this stuff up."